ACKNOWLEDGEME

First I would like to thank my wife Haylee, for her support through the process of this book.

I want to thank Beverly Hill, for helping with the formatting.

And I'd like to thank Paul Hill, from ArtsyLaser, for the layout, and design of the cover.

Bound for Carnage

BY

Patrick Langridge

My eyes felt really heavy like I hadn't slept in a long time. managing to get up, I leant against a wall. Now I could see a little, I recognised the alley I was standing in. Confused, looking around the alleyway, there was nobody around. I remembered having a briefcase, but where was it? I was walking through this alleyway when I felt a sharp stabbing in my neck, next thing I knew I was waking up on the floor. My head still wasn't clear. I walked cautiously to the end of the alley way. Looking left and right, down the street, everyone was going about their business. I was just a few streets away from my apartment, so I went back home. After getting cleaned up I sat on the edge of my bed trying to remember what happened. My memory was still a little fuzzy. What the hell happened? Someone wanted that case, but why? Lying down, I closed my eyes and drifted off. The following morning, I still had no idea as to what was going on. I'd obviously been jumped, but by who? someone who knew what I was carrying? Or a random attack? Either way, I still couldn't remember what was in the briefcase. It's just as if I'd left my apartment yesterday, and lost my memory. Although I knew where I lived, I don't seem to remember much else. My head was throbbing so I went into the kitchen to take some pain killers. After pouring myself a mug of strong black

4

coffee, I sat on the couch trying to remember something, anything. I decided to go for a walk, the fresh air might clear my head. It was a bright day outside; the sun was low and warm. After a few minutes, I approached the alleyway that I woke up in the previous evening. I looked down the alleyway, trying to visualise what had happened to me. I Just couldn't seem to remember what happened. I decided to call a good friend of mine, John. He's more like a brother. We've known each other for years. we met in the military and have been friends ever since. He has a wife, Sally, and twin daughters, Charlotte and Georgina. John answered.

"Alright mate how's things?"

"Not great mate to be honest, can we meet up?"

"Sally and the girls are going out in a few minutes so we can talk here in peace. That good for you?"

"Perfect mate be there soon".

I ended the call, and went back to get my car.

I arrived at John's house around ten thirty. Sally and the girls weren't there. I knocked on the door and John answered.

"Good to see you mate"

"You too mate"

I followed him inside and into the living room.

"Want some coffee"?

"That'll be great thanks"

I took a seat on the sofa whilst he went to make the coffee.

"So, what's up with you"? John said, as he passed me my coffee.

I took a sip of the coffee and told him what I knew about the previous 24 hours.

"So where were you going with this case?"

"No idea. I remember having it, but don't know what was in it or where I was taking it, but it's gone because someone took it. I just need to find out who. I've obviously been given this case for a reason but by who? Why?"

"I'm not sure how you intend to figure all of this out but you need to start remembering"

"Tell me about it "

"Maybe you were drugged. That would explain the memory loss thing"

"It's possible" I said.

"I mean think about it, you can remember everything before having the briefcase and waking up in that alleyway. Hopefully you'll remember more soon so we can figure out why you had it and what was in it. Then maybe we can start piecing this together."

"I'm going to head home and try to figure this out."

"Ok mate, I'll see if I can come up with anything."

I arrived back home and switched the coffee machine on. Then I went into the living room and turned my laptop on, whilst that was starting up, I went back into the kitchen to pour myself a coffee, and I heard the laptop ping telling me I had a notification. It was a new email, so I opened it up. There was no sender information. Just a message that read....

COSTA COFFEE SHOP

KINGS CROSS STATION

TOMORROW MORNING 10 AM

BRING OVERNIGHT BAG

DON'T BE LATE

What the hell is this all about I thought. I called John and told him about the message.

"You going?" He asked.

"May get some answers"

 "You don't know who sent that message. You don't know what will happen when you get there, and an overnight bag, what's that all about?"

 "Only one way to find out"

"Maybe I should come with you"

"If you are with me, it may complicate things. Anyway, I may need you back here".

"Be careful mate. Keep in touch with me, so I know what's going on"

"I will mate."

I ended the call and poured myself another coffee. Then I read the message again...

COSTA COFFEE SHOP

KINGS CROSS STATION

TOMORROW MORNING 10 AM

BRING OVERNIGHT BAG

DON'T BE LATE

4

An unknown man was sitting on a wooden bench Reading a newspaper. Every now and then he would look towards the Costa coffee shop, a brief glance, but taking it all in. He had been sitting there since nine-thirty just reading and watching. The time now was nine- fifty and he noticed a man out of the corner of his eye walk towards the Costa Coffee shop, with a bag over his shoulder. He continued to watch the man without making it look obvious. The man ordered himself a coffee and went and sat down outside the Costa shop.

The unknown man continued to read his newspaper until it was precisely ten o'clock. He then folded his newspaper and stood up. He put his newspaper under his arm and started walking over to the guy at the Costa shop. The guy at the Costa looked up just as the unknown man got to his table. "Your name," said the unknown man.

"Mike" said the guy.

"Follow me"

Mike stood up, put his bag back over his shoulder grabbed his coffee and followed the unknown man. Mike followed him to a darker quieter spot in the station. Once there the unknown man stopped, turned around and pulled out an envelope from inside his jacket and handed it to Mike.

"Inside this envelope are some tickets for a train. The train you need to be on, is the ten- thirty from St Pancras station to Heathrow Airport. You have a seat on a mid-afternoon flight to Los Angeles. All the details are in here, plus everything you will need, money, ID passport. Go to the address detailed in here, and wait for someone to contact you".

"Who. Who will contact me, what the hell is going on?"

"Just get to that address and wait, we know about the briefcase, we can help."

The unknown man walked away.

5

In my line of work this sort of thing can happen from time to time but it's never happened to me until now. I'm what you could call a clandestine transporter. I get goods from A to B secretly. Secret papers, valuable objects, anything small that needs moving.

I needed to get the case and its contents back no matter what. I opened the envelope, and checked the contents. It all seemed to be there. I put the envelope in my jacket pocket, and made my way over to St Pancras station. After finding out which platform I needed, I took a seat, and decided to call John. I got my phone out of my pocket, but changed my mind. I'd wait until I got to where I was going. The train to Heathrow pulled in, I boarded the train and grabbed a seat in a corner out of the way. 56 minutes later the train pulled into Heathrow Airport, I got off the train and made my way over to Terminal 5. My flight was due to board at 1500 hrs, so I had time to get something to eat and drink.

Once I'd eaten, I went to check in then grabbed a seat and looked through the envelope again. Looking through the details, I noticed I had Hertz paperwork for a hire car when I got to LA. There was a key for an apartment in Santa Monica. The loud speaker in the departures lounge announced that the plane I was waiting for was now boarding. I placed the envelope back in my jacket pocket, keeping the passport and boarding pass in my hand ready to board. I boarded the plane and found my seat. It was a window seat, which was fine with me. I planned to sleep as much as I could, because I didn't know what I was getting into in LA. A middle-aged man took the aisle seat next to me, leaving the middle Seat between us free. We exchanged small talk then we were asked to put our seatbelts on ready to taxi to the runway. Eventually we took off and got up to altitude. The steward brought round the drinks trolley. I turned down the drinks trolley and shut my eyes because I wanted to get some shut eye before food came round.

About an hour later the food trolley came round and I had what I thought was a decent pasta meal washed down with a small cup of half decent coffee, then it was time to get my head down again.

6

I was woken up and asked to buckle up ready for landing. After we landed, I made my way to arrivals. Once through I made my way over to the Hertz car hire building. After going through all the paperwork, I was handed the keys to a Chevy suburban. I put the address of the apartment into the GPS and drove out of the car park. I arrived at my destination on Olympic Drive, Santa Monica after a longer than meant to be journey. I finally found a spot to park the Chevy and walked round to the apartment. After letting myself in I had a look around to get a feel for the place. There were Some essentials in the cupboards and fridge. I put the kettle on to make a coffee. Deciding not to unpack my bag in case I had to leave in a hurry, I drank the coffee then went for a shower. It was now eight PM. So, 4am UK time. So, I decided to try and get some sleep.

I was eventually woken up by my phone chirping a message.

WILL BE WITH YOU IN TEN MINUTES.

By this point it was two AM, LA time. I went and rinsed my face and got dressed. Hearing a knock on the door, I looked through the peep hole and saw a tall looking man with short dark hair and wearing John Lennon style glasses. And wearing what looked like a leather motorcycle jacket. "What do you want?" I said.

"My name is Richard; I am your contact."

"Then tell me why you are here"

"Because you lost a briefcase"

I opened the door and Richard stepped inside. As I closed the door behind him, I said...

"For the record, I didn't lose it. It was taken"

"It doesn't matter how it vanished, all that matters now is getting it back. I'm going to make this quick so please listen to what I have to say. That briefcase contains Sensitive documents and photos. I'm not going to go into too much detail right now, but I can tell you that the case has, or at least, had a GPS tracker inside. The problem we have now is, the GPS tracker has stopped working. We believe the signal has been jammed somehow. We followed it to LA, once it left the airport, we lost it".

"Well, that's that then it's gone. what do you need me for?"

"It's now two thirty-five AM. You will be picked up at nine AM, so be ready."

"You need to tell me exactly what's going on"

"Later on, today you will know all you need to know."

After Richard left, I messaged John to let him know what was going on, then I got my head down again.

7

John walked to the kitchen to pour himself a coffee. As he poured his coffee, he received a text from mike:

ALL SETTLED THIS END. GETTING PICKED UP LATER, TO GO WHERE? I DONT KNOW. WILL BE IN TOUCH.

After reading the message he replied:

OK MATE KEEP SAFE CHAT SOON.

John then went and switched on his laptop. Once the laptop had started up; he sent an email to a private investigator by the name of William Selmonns, a 61-year-old gent from London, who now lives in the Kent countryside of Godden Green, near Sevenoaks. John and William have worked together on a couple of jobs in the past. John ran a security business, mainly from home. They have shared information with each other on occasion. In the email, John asked William if he had any unsolved cases recently that he would class as secretive. John sent the email then went to the kitchen to pour himself another coffee. Johns' thoughts were, if someone went to the trouble of possibly drugging Mike and stealing the briefcase, then whatever was in the case must be really important to somebody. After a couple of hours work and drinking coffee, John received an email from William:

HELLO JOHN, I HAVE NOTHING OUTSTANDING AT THE MOMENT. I HAVE SOME EVIDENCE BEING TRANSPORTED TO THE STATES AS WE SPEAK. MURDERER FOR HIRE THING. THATS IT RIGHT NOW. ALL THE BEST, WILL.

John read the email and replied: OK WILL. THANKS FOR GETTING BACK TO ME. KIND REGARDS, JOHN.

John went and fixed himself some lunch then went back to his office. Whilst eating and working, a thought occurred to him. He emailed William again:

HI WILL, I REALISE YOU CAN'T GO INTO DETAIL ABOUT YOUR FINDINGS, BUT YOU SAY YOU HAVE EVIDENCE ON ITS WAY TO THE STATES NOW. THAT EVIDENCE WOULDN'T HAPPEN TO BE IN A BRIEFCASE, WOULD IT?

THANKS, JOHN.

HI JOHN, STRANGE QUESTION, BUT YES IT WOULD. WHY DO YOU ASK?   WILL.

John read Williams reply, and decided to call him instead.

"Hi John, will said. Care to enlighten me?"

"Hi Will, yes sorry to bother you. I have a friend who transports goods on the QT. He has recently had an item taken from him, after we believe, being drugged."

"Let me guess. This item was in a briefcase?".

"Exactly that. This friend received an anonymous message instructing him to go to King's Cross Station. Now he is in LA"

"When did this happen" said Will.

"He flew out yesterday from Heathrow."

"I received confirmation three days ago, that the case had been handed over to a transporter. I'm still waiting for confirmation it's been delivered to its final destination"

"Well, my guess is, you won't be seeing that confirmation anytime soon"

"OK, we need to talk. Can you come here?"

"OK" said John. "see you in a couple of hours"

"Excellent, see you soon"

8

10.30 AM LOS ANGELES

I woke up, showered, and got dressed. Whilst eating my breakfast I decided to send John a message:

HI JOHN. IM GETTING PICKED UP IN HALF AN HOUR. I WILL CONTACT YOU, FIRST CHANCE I GET, AND LET YOU KNOW WHATS HAPPENING.

After a couple of minutes, I got a call from him.

"Hi John, how's things"

"Hello mate," said John. "I'll make this quick, as you are being picked up soon".

"Ok, go on"

"I've just had an interesting chat with a friend of mine. It appears that the case that was taken from you, could very well be holding evidence in a murderer for hire case he's been working on. He received confirmation that the case was handed over to a transporter, 3 days ago. He has been waiting for final destination confirmation since."

"You think his case, was the case I had?"

"We believe so. The people I'm dealing with here know about the missing case and want to help get it back"

"Just be careful, it's possible the husband knows about the evidence and wants to get his hands on it before it gets out. He stands to lose everything so he may do whatever it takes to keep it from getting out".

"So, it's a rich wife thing. The people I'm meeting over here, must be working for the wife. I will see what they have to say, and get back to you."

"Ok, watch your back Mike. Call me if you need me"

"Will do mate, chat soon."

I ended the call as there was a knock on the door. "Hello" I said. "I'm your eleven o'clock pick-up" said the guy on the other side of the door.

"I'll be there in a minute"

The guy walked back to his vehicle. I checked that I had my things and left the apartment. The guy had the rear passenger door open for me. As I slipped onto the back seat, he closed the door. After the guy got into the driver's seat and pulled away from the parking space, I asked him where we were going.

"Someone wants to see you. It's not too far away"

I didn't bother with anymore conversation because the guy didn't seem as though he wanted to chat.

9

After about twenty minutes we arrived at a big set of gates on a hill. The gates opened and we drove up to a big house. We pulled up at the foot of some steps leading up to the front door. There stood a big pillar either side of the door, and the door was surrounded by windows, and the outside of the house was cladded in blue. The guy opened my door and I stepped out of the vehicle. As I turned to look up the steps, the door opened. A man with greying hair, wearing suit trousers and a shirt open at the neck called out to me.

"Hello Mr Prowling, so pleased to meet you"

"Who might you be?" I said, as I climbed the steps.

"You can call me Stan" he said as he offered me his hand to shake. "Welcome to Los Angeles."

I Followed him inside the house. There was a big entrance hallway with high ceilings, and stairs leading off left and right from a central staircase. We took a left before the stairs, and entered a room which was a library / office. The door closed behind us, leaving just Stan and I in the room.

"Please, take a seat" he said pointing to a pair of armchairs. "Can I get you a drink?"

"Just water for me please"

I took a seat in one of the armchairs as Stan came over with my water. After handing me my drink, he took a seat on the sofa opposite.

"So, Mr Prowling. I brought you here so we can help each other. Something was taken from you, and we really need to get it back."

"I'm not sure how I can be of any help" I said.

"Can you tell me where you got the case from?"

"I get paid to transport the goods. I get handed the goods, and instructions telling me where the goods need to get to. I don't always know what I'm carrying, I just get the goods to where they need to be, then my job is done."

"Do you know what you were carrying this time?"

I decided to play it down for now, see where the conversation went.

"No idea" I said. "I was handed the case with instructions where to take it"

"And where were you instructed to take it?"

"An address near San Francisco. I don't recall the exact address".

"Are you in the habit of forgetting an address?"

23

"NO. I believe I was drugged when the case was taken. They would have had a hard time getting it from me otherwise. I had a little memory loss after waking up after it was taken. It's the only explanation I have"

I could remember the full address just fine. In fact, my memory was fine by this point, but I wasn't going to give much away right then. I didn't know who these people were.

"I see. Well here is something you might not be aware of. The contents you were carrying in that case is evidence that a man by the name of Rufus Longson had his wife's father killed. His wife believes he had her father killed a few years ago in London. We know she contacted a private investigator over there, and we now know that the evidence was in the form of photos and a memory stick. We don't know if the stick holds a recording of the meeting or some other proof, but Mrs Longson needs that evidence before she can do anything about it" "What's this Rufus guy have to say about all this?"

 "No one has spoken to him about this yet. His wife needs the evidence first before she confronts him."

"So, what next? You flew me out here, so I assume you have a plan"

"We want you to transport another case. Identical to the one that was taken from you. We want Rufus to think there is another set of evidence, then catch him trying to get it back".

"Where is this new case to be taken"

"It's more of a wild goose chase, we have put a GPS tracker in the case, and they won't find this one. We are hoping this will lead us to where the other evidence was taken. Hopefully allowing us to get the real case back".

"You want me to let them take it"

"Yes. But not until we tell you to. You will fly to New York, then you will be given a vehicle and the case, then you will drive it back to San Francisco. Only you won't have it by then, but we need this to play out as normal as possible until it's taken from you. It's easier for us to track and help you this way. Then we follow the case."

"This seems a long-winded way of doing it. Why don't you just grab this Rufus guy and deal with him?"

"It's easier for us this way, things are more easily dealt with on the ground, we can't let him know that we are onto him. We are hoping he hasn't destroyed the evidence yet, Danny here will take you back to your apartment. He has everything you need. Money, tickets. We will have a weapon for you the other end"

"I don't use weapons; I'm not going to be shooting anybody"

"Just for protection," said Stan. "Here is a phone for you, you can call me and Danny if you need anything. We will be tracking you, so we will know where you are at all times, just precautionary"

Stan handed me the phone and I put it in my pocket.

"I guess I'll be in touch" I said.

"Good luck, Mike"

We shook hands, then I followed Danny back out to his vehicle.

John pulled up to Williams countryside property, after parking his car on the small driveway, he walked over to the front door and knocked. He waited a few moments then knocked again. No answer. He called out to William, no answer. He banged harder on the door with his fist and it came ajar. John slowly pushed the door open and called William again. Still no answer. Just then he heard a door shut, not loud, just a faint click of the latch. John walked through the house, towards the back door where the noise had come from calling William as he went, still no answer. Then he spotted a man in the back garden, running towards the back fence. He was wearing jeans, a short black jacket, and a motorcycle helmet. John opened the back door and shouted after him. The man jumped up, and climbed over the fence.

John ran across the garden towards the back fence, as he got near the fence, he heard a motorcycle engine start up and then pull away. John climbed up the fence and looked over in time to see the back of the rider disappear into the trees. John climbed back down and ran towards the house, and in through the back door. He called out for William again as he checked downstairs, not finding him, he ran upstairs and checked the bathroom. Then he checked the bedroom.

He then went to the only other room upstairs, a second bedroom that was being used as an office/library. Straight ahead was a big desk with a window behind it. To the right a couple of book shelves, and on the wall behind the door, a couple of filing cabinets. John walked into the room, past the filing cabinets and round the end of the desk. That's where he saw a slipper covered foot, and as he carried on round the desk he saw the rest of William's body. There was a pool of blood around his head and a deep cut to his throat. John swore out load and stood there stunned for a moment. Finally, he snapped out of it. He went to the bathroom to get some tissue, he wrapped it around his hand and picked up the office phone. He called the police and told them what he'd found, leaving no details about himself. he ended the call. "Sorry buddy" he said out loud. He then left the house walked to his car and drove away from the property. He took a slightly longer route home so he could think. After arriving home and greeting his wife, he walked to his office and closed the door. The girls were already in bed as it was now ten PM. He poured himself a big glass of rum, and sat down heavy in his chair. He sat there for a short while just shocked at what he'd found when he went to Will's house. He downed his drink and got up and poured another. John didn't drink much, but tonight he needed something. He decided to message Mike, telling him to call him asap. He then downed his drink and poured another. Then his wife Sally came in and asked if he was ok and said that she was going to go up to bed with a book.

"I'll be up in a little while" he said.

She kissed him then left the room. John didn't know what to do next, so he decided to wait until he had spoken with Mike and take it from there.

11

KENT

A man on a motorcycle pulled into a layby. He pulled his phone from his pocket and Dialled a number. When that call was answered he simply said "Job done".

The voice on the other end of the line replied "ok good". Then the call ended.

The motorcyclist put his phone away and pulled out of the layby and carried on with his journey.

At that moment, back in Los Angeles, I was dropped off at my apartment back on Olympic drive. After my meeting with Stan, I had Danny take me via a department store, and a McDonald's before taking me home. I wanted to get some fresh clothes and some food. The overnight bag I came here with wouldn't be enough now I had to travel around a bit.

After letting myself in and dumping my bags on my bed, I went and sat down with the McDonald's. Just then my phone chirped at me, alerting me to a message. A message from John.

CALL ME ASAP. URGENT.

I called him straight away, it was now eleven PM UK, but he'd said URGENT so I didn't wait. John answered on the second ring.

"Mike There's been a situation this end".

"Ok mate, what's wrong"

"That friend of mine, the one who found the evidence that was taken. He's dead. Someone cut his throat. It was a bloody mess Mike, I've seen some shit in my life? but this was on another level"

"Shit. Sorry mate, this obviously goes way deeper than we first thought."

"He asked me to go over there because he said we needed to talk. When I got into the house, a guy left by the back door, jumped over the fence, and got away on a motorcycle."

"Did you get the registration"

"No ,by the time I got up the fence he was away through the trees".

"Someone clearly knows what your friend was onto, you need to distance yourself from this John. You have a family at home."

"No way. I'm going to find out who did this, and why".

"You need to keep Sally and the girl's safe mate, let me deal with this, it's my mess".

"Not anymore, I'm involved now, and I won't rest until I find that son of a bitch. I will get Sally and the girls away from here, then I'm going to figure this out. What's happening your end?"

"I'm flying out to New York tomorrow, they want me to drive across to San Francisco with a fake case, hoping the bad guys, whoever they are, will try and get it. We are making it look like we have some other evidence, and are taking it to where the original case was meant to go. It'll be tracked by GPS, and they have given me a phone which they can also track, so it should all be fine".

"You need to be careful mate. This is going to get out of hand."

"You just keep yourself and the girls safe, and I'll be in touch soon"

Not long after ending the call with John, I received a message from Stan telling me I was being picked up at six thirty AM and to be ready. I spent the rest of the day watching the TV, mainly the news and thought about John for a while too. He lost a friend because of this situation and I felt for him. We've both lost friends before, when we we're in the military together. Seen friends lose body parts from IEDs. We've been through shit together, but finding a friend with his throat cut open was something else. I decide to get my head down early. The next few days were going to be long, so any sleep I got beforehand was going to help.

I woke up to my alarm chirping at five thirty the next morning, had a shower and got dressed, then I went and made myself coffee and breakfast. After eating and finishing my coffee I checked my gear to make sure I had everything. As I was finishing my second coffee there was a knock at the door. I looked through the peephole to see Danny my driver waiting outside. I grabbed my gear and followed Danny to the car. After getting in and setting off, Danny passed me an envelope.

"This contains the things you need."

I opened it to check the contents. More money, looked like a couple of grand in tens and twenties. Hire car information. "No apartment this time "? I asked, sarcastically.

"You will have to sort out your own stop overs as and when you need to" said Danny.

After a twenty-minute drive, we arrived at the airport.

"Contact us if you need anything" said Danny.

I got out of the car and made my way to terminal 5, wondering how the next few days were going to pan out. I planned to get across to San Francisco in three to four days. That's if I ended up going that far, depends on when the case is taken and what Stan's plans are.

I got through check-in and had an hour to kill before my flight. I went to get some breakfast and coffee. Once I was done eating I went over to the boarding gate. I eventually boarded the plane, and once we were in the air and cruising, I shut my eyes. I knew I probably wouldn't get any more sleep, but the rest would help. After an uneventful flight we landed at JFK. Once through arrivals I went to pick up my car from the car hire firm. After being handed the keys to a blue Dodge Ram, I went to the truck and phoned Stan. I asked him where I was picking up the case. He told me to go to the BP station off highway eighty just outside city of Orange. After a little over an hour I arrived at the BP station services car park. I was met by a guy who handed me the briefcase. He told me the weapon was inside the case, to hide it somewhere in the truck. We parted company, and I drove back out onto highway eighty. This was the start of my journey. I needed to keep an eye out for possible pursuers. I needed to be alert, and ready for anything.

It was around five PM, I was driving on highway eighty. I decided to stick to the main route. It would give me more options if I need to take another route for any reason. I would give it a few more hours then find a room for the night. I was sticking to the speed limits just taking my time. After a little while I noticed a vehicle in the rear view mirror that had been following me for a while now. Is this it? I thought to myself. Is this the start of it all? I drove for a further half hour or so, with the vehicle still following. I needed to get off the highway and see if they followed, if so I need to lose them. A turn off for a place called Berwick was a mile and a half away, I would turn off there and see what the vehicle did. I took the slip off highway eighty and the vehicle continued to follow. I Drove over the Susquehanna river into Berwick. I didn't know this area so I just took a few left and right turns. They continued to follow. They weren't trying to hide the fact they were following me. They were no more than seventy or eighty yards behind. Whoever these people were, they didn't care about alerting me to their presence. They obviously didn't mind getting onto altercations. I needed to stop this now. I turned down a track, then saw a sign telling me this leads to a dead end. I guess this was where it was going to go down. I pulled over to the side, not completely blocking the track. I cut the engine, jumped out of the truck and run behind some low bushes. It was dark, apart from the light bouncing around from their headlights. I watched as they pulled up behind my truck. I heard two doors open, but not close again. They weren't planning on hanging around. I saw two silhouettes slowly walk towards my truck. Their car was behind them. I couldn't make out too much with their car lights shining my way. I needed to act now. I walked out of the bushes doing up my zipper, as if I'd been peeing.

"Alright lads" I said, loud enough to get their attention.

They both stopped and looked in my direction. I still couldn't make out much in the light. I walked towards the truck as one of the guys was about to try the door. I pressed the fob so it locked. Lights flashed to confirm it had done what I had asked of it. The guy still tried the door to no avail. That guy continued round that side of the truck while his mate stayed this side walking towards me. The guy nearest me says,

"The best thing you can do is give us what we want, and no one has to get hurt".

Wow, I thought, straight down to business. These guys looked ready to fight to get what they wanted, no doubt about it. I needed to get in there first. I needed to take down the nearest guy before his mate was close enough to help him. I took a step towards him. He doesn't move. I take a step closer, and he got ready to take a stand. I dropped low, spun and kicked his legs from underneath him. He drops to the floor as I started running towards the other guy. I needed to keep them separated as long as possible. I ran at the other guy full steam. I was practically on top of him when he crouched, and with his full body weight threw me over his shoulders. I landed hard, and was winded. The guy wasted no time getting to me, and started raining down punches. His mate then joined him. This had not gone how I had expected. This guy was bigger than his mate, and I could feel it in the blows I was receiving. I curled up and tried to protect myself. After what seemed like a lifetime, a shot rang out. The beating stopped and the guys stood up.

"You need to take your problems somewhere else. You don't have permission to be on this land".

"Get lost" said one of the guys standing over me. "Mind your business".

Another shot rang out, kicking up dirt about two metres away from where we were.

"I said go somewhere else, or the next shot will be aimed at you" said the guy with the gun.

"ok, chill" said one of the guys standing over me.

As the two guys walked away, one of them stuck the boot in. "see you soon" he said.

They went back to their vehicle, did a U turn and sped off, kicking up dust everywhere. I stood up, slowly, coughing, spitting out blood. I could still feel all of my teeth, so nothing missing there. And nothing else seemed to be broken. Pain came from various parts of me, but I was alive, so that was good.

"Thanks" I said.

The guy with the gun said "Get in your truck and leave. And don't come back here."

I hobbled to the truck, got in very slowly and painfully. Getting as comfortable as I could, I start the truck, did a U turn, all the time being watched by the guy with the gun. Then I drove away.

It was getting late. I was back on highway eighty. There was no sign of those guys yet. They were out there, waiting to pounce again. I was aching all over and needed to get cleaned up and rest. The next town was Clearfield, it looked like a small enough place to lose myself in. I pulled of the highway and looked for somewhere I could get cleaned up and get some food. There was a Walmart was still open, so I pull in to the car park and found a parking spot near the entrance. I walked inside and got some funny looks, because I was covered in dirt, and had dried blood in places. I asked where the toilets were, and a staff member pointed the way. I got cleaned up as best I could, then I went and grabbed some food and bottles of water. After paying for the goods I went back out to the truck, looking around, I couldn't see any suspicious looking vehicles, or the guys I'd met earlier. I climbed slowly in to the truck, most joints aching from the effort, and pull out of the car park. I looked for somewhere quiet and dark to park up in, not wanting to use a motel. I needed to keep out of the way, somewhere those thugs wouldn't bother me. I soon found a disused building surrounded by some fencing. Warning signs were telling people to stay out. Looks like a good place to hide the truck so I could get some rest. A chain and padlock was holding the fencing shut, but the brackets holding the panels together looked like they could be nudged loose. I found a brick on the floor and start hitting one of the brackets until it came loose, managing to free up the bracket I pulled the fence apart enough to drive the truck through. I pulled through the fence then pulled the fence panels back together. Then I drove round the back of the building. Its was darker there, so it should be a good spot to park up. I then got out and just stood there for a couple of minutes listening. I heard nothing telling me there was anyone around, so I got some food down my neck and washed it down with some water. Once I'd eaten I climbed into the back seat, making sure the case and the gun were within easy reach. I messaged Stan to let him know what was going on, then got as comfortable as I could and got my head down.

15

0600 HRS   LONDON

John got out of bed, went down stairs and switched on the coffee machine. He hardly slept despite the alcohol he drank before going to bed. He still couldn't believe what had happened to will. He then went and switched on his laptop. After getting back to his office with a fresh coffee he shut the door and sat heavy in his office chair. I need to find out who killed Will, he said to himself with a sigh. He didn't know where to start. After a few minutes thinking, he went onto Will's private Investigators website. Not much there to see, just numbers and an email address to contact him. There were two phone numbers, he tried them both and got no answer. He didn't know if Will had someone dealing with his website. John sent an email to the email address, requesting someone to transport some goods. Worth a shot, he thought. He then spent sometime searching the net but couldn't find anything helpful. He decided to message Mike and see how he was doing. It is now eight AM, so it would be midnight in LA. He will get the message in the morning at least. He sent the message then went upstairs to shower. John had spent all day yesterday pretty much just moping around the house after he convinced Sally to take the girls to her mothers for a few days. After the shower he poured himself another coffee, then took that to his office. He noticed he had a new email so he opened it and read it.

THIS OFFICE IS TEMPORARILY CLOSED FOR BUSINESS. IF YOU WISH TO SPEAK TO SOMEONE REFERENCE YOUR REQUEST, PLEASE CALL THE NUMBER BELOW.

John dialled the number, and it was answered after the second ring.

"Hi" said a male voice on the other end.

"Hello" said John. "I'm calling because I have a package I need delivering".

"No problem, we can meet and discuss it"

"Excellent. I need it delivering asap." Said John.

"I will send you the address. I'm here until late, so we can chat today if that's good for you?"

John thanked the man and ended the call. A few seconds later he received the address. No time like the present he thought. This can't be normal procedure, John thought. Especially as the business is closed. John left to meet this man. He didn't trust this situation one bit. But this could maybe lead to something useful in finding out why Will was killed. After an hour and twenty-minute ride, John turned down a dirt track leading to an old farm. He parked his vehicle at the side of the track and walked the rest of the way. He wanted to check out the area quietly first. He kept to the grass verge and walked carefully towards the farm. He eventually came up to the farm main entrance. A main house was just ahead, and there were other out buildings dotted about. He walked slowly towards the main house, scanning the area as he went. The house didn't look like it had been lived in for a while. John wasn't happy about seeing this through but he needed to. He needed to get some answers, and this was where he would start. He walked up to the door to the house, and instead of knocking, he turned the handle slowly and the door clicked open. The door hinges squeaked a little as he pushed the door open. There was a short hallway in front of him. A door to the left and right, both closed. He tried the door on the left, it was locked. The one on the right came open as he tried it. John walked slowly into the room, and heard a creaking noise behind him. As he looked round, his world went dark.

16

0630 HRS LOS ANGELES

I woke up and sat up slowly, still aching from the beating I received. It all seemed quiet as I looked around outside. Slowly I dragged myself out of the truck wincing as I moved. I stood and stretched trying to loosen myself up a bit. Splashed my face with water then drank some. As I messaged Stan to let him know I would soon be starting the next leg of my journey, I noticed I had a message from John asking how things were going. I messaged him back and told him about my encounter the previous night. I then sorted myself out and made my way out of the fencing, closing it behind me. Driving back to highway eighty I received a call from Stan.

"Hello"

"Hi Mike. I have a couple of guys coming your way. They will follow you from a distance. Let the case go next time you have an encounter with those men. My guys will follow them and see where they go"

"Ok " I said.

The call ended. I just needed to drive now, and let them find me. Then the case is someone else's problem. I received a message from Stan, telling me to head to San Francisco anyway once the case had been taken.

After a few hours I found a truck stop and had a big meal and got some fresh supplies for the journey. Once Back on the road I felt full and a little more relaxed. After a little while I kept my eye on a car that had been following me for a few miles. I carried on a while longer and it still followed. It looks like there were two people in the vehicle, but it was too far away to be sure. It was that time again. Time to turn off this road and see if they follow. A sign for Angola Indiana was soon coming up on highway ninety. Soon I turned off for Angola highway twenty. The car was still following. It was a Ford Focus. Two guys in it. They were closer now and not bothered about me knowing they were there. I saw a sign for Fox Lake. This will do I thought. I turned down a small road towards the lake trying to keep away from the more public areas. I parked off the road under some trees. After stepping out of the truck I put the gun into the waistband of my jeans. I then walked into the trees and watched, moments later I heard an engine and the Ford Focus came into view and parked a little way back from my truck. The guy's both got out and walked either side of my truck. As they got alongside the truck I stepped out from the trees.

"You don't give up do you?" I said.

They both turned to look at me. Smiling, one of them said...

 "Oh, look our little friend wants to play again"

His mate laughed at this.

"Not this time" I said.

"I will give you what you want if you tell me who wants it"

"That's of no concern to you. We will be taking it with or without your permission".

"No, you won't" I said, pulling out the gun and pointing it at him. The smaller of the two, was standing the other side of the truck. He pulled out his gun and pointed at me.

"Looks like we have a problem"

"No problem on my side. I'm keeping the case".

I knew I had to give it to them this time, but it had to look like I was going to try and keep it.

A few seconds passed, and the sound of another engine came towards us. A ford pickup then appeared and pulled up behind the ford focus. Two men stepped out and drew weapons, pointing them at the guys from the focus. I did not see this coming. One of the new guys told the other two to put down their weapons. The guy behind my truck refused, keeping his weapon aimed at me. The next sound I heard was a muffled pop, and the big guy from the Ford Focus hit the floor with a chunk of his head missing. His mate ducked down behind my truck. I ran behind the nearest tree. No idea what was going on.

"Mike" one of them shouted. I peeked round the tree to see one of the new guys looking at me. "Stan sent us"

I felt myself relax a bit. I stepped out from the tree, gun still up. "Why did you shoot him?" I asked.

"Just worry about the other one"

The other bad guy was still behind my truck. The new guys slowly walk towards the truck, guns raised. The bad guy suddenly jumped up and fired He missed his target as a bullet took out one of his eyes. The guy who shot him walked over and put two more in his head.

"They were supposed to take the case. Stan told you that right?"

"No one is taking the case" he said. He pointed his gun at his partner and shot him in the head, blowing brain and bone across the floor. I aimed my gun at him. "What the hell are you doing?"

"I'm the only one walking away with this case" he said.

Then he took a shot at me as I dived for cover. I heard a window smash, then he put his arm in my truck and grabbed the case. I took a shot at him, missing. He works his way towards his truck, firing blindly in my direction. He's just keeping my head down so I couldn't shoot at him. I let off a couple of shots in his direction, not really seeing where they went. Then I heard his truck revving up. I ran out of the tree line taking pot shots at him as he reversed at speed and disappeared. Why did he do this? Who's side was he on?

17

2200HRS NEAR DORKING SURREY

John opened his eyes. He was in an empty room tied to a chair. His hands were tingling because they were tied up so tight. The only light in the room was from a gap in the window where a wooden slat was missing. His head was throbbing where he'd been hit over the head.

"Hello" he called. No answer. "Hello" he shouted. Still nothing. He tried to work his hands free, but that didn't happen. Just then the door opened and a man, tall with stubble on his chin, wearing jeans and a short black jacket walked in carrying a tin mug.

"Hello John. Nice to see you are awake"

John didn't answer. The man put the tin mug filled with water to John's lips, and he knocked it away with his chin.

"Don't be foolish," said the man. "you won't be offered anymore". "Who are you? what do you want?"

"Ah, straight down to business I see. Very well. I want to know about your friend Mike."

"I don't have any friends by that name," said John.

"You have a friend by the name of Mike, currently in the U.S. And I'd like to know what he is up to"

"No, I don't"

"Don't play games John. I will get this information from you whether you give it up freely, Or I get it from you. So, tell me. What is he up to?"

"No idea"

Then a punch to his face made him see stars. He took the punch well so as not to look weak in front of this man.

"You are going to suffer if you do not tell me what I want to know"

"Go to hell," said John. Then he spat blood on the man's boots. He received a hard back handed slap for that comment.

"This will only get worse for you John"

"At least tell me who you are" said John.

"You can call me, Nick. Now tell me what Mike is doing in the U.S."

"Probably on vacation for all I know. I haven't spoken to him in a while."

"I know you have been speaking with him recently. Don't test my patience, John. Answer the damn question. What is he up to?"

"Don't know" said John.

Before he knew what was happening, Nick had him by the throat and forced him backwards until he hit the floor still tied to the chair. He squeezed John's throat until John went bright red and started to struggle. Then he let go and simply walked out of the room. John laid there tied up on the floor, chair underneath him, catching his breath. He needed to find a way out of this. Fast.

18

1830 HRS. GENESEO IL

I contacted Stan, after the shit storm in Angola. I told him that one of his guys has the briefcase. He hadn't told the guys he sent out to me, that the case was a decoy. He must have taken it, planning on selling it to the highest bidder, thinking it contained more evidence. Stan asked me to keep heading over to San Francisco, to where Rufus lives. The case is being tracked, so they can keep an eye on where it's heading. The guy would at some point, no doubt contact Stan or Rufus to try and sell them the case. I would just make my way across country. I hadn't heard anymore from John. I try calling him then realised it was only two thirty AM in the UK. I hung up and decide to try again later after I'd driven for a few more hours. It will be a decent time in the UK then. I hoped he would find his friend's killer but I was hoping he wouldn't do anything stupid.

19

0230 HRS. DORKING SURREY UK

John woke up lying on the floor, still tied to the chair, he was really thirsty now. His arms were numb from being trapped between the chair and the floor. He tried to rock the chair and roll onto his side, but he struggled to. He needed to take the pressure off. Nick would soon return, so he wanted his arms working, even if they were tied up. He kept trying to roll over but it was no use. He put too much pressure on his shoulders every time he tried. The door opened and in walked Nick. He had the tin mug again. He put down the tin mug and helped John back into an upright position. He then offered the mug up to John's lips. John swallowed all the water down. He could feel his arms starting to tingle as the blood started coming back with the pressure now taken off. Nick opened the door and grabbed a chair that was outside in the hallway. He put the chair in front of John, a few feet away.

"Well John, I hope you've had enough time to think about your predicament, shall we start this again? I think we got off on the wrong foot".

John said nothing.

"Come on John, talk to me. Make this easy on yourself. Tell me what I want to know and you will walk free."

"You haven't gone to all this trouble, just to let me walk away."

"This was no trouble John. I have nothing personal against you.

I just want some answers. Tell me, and you won't see me again".

"Bullshit" said John.

"Don't be like that"

"I've already told you. I don't know"

Nick sat there clenching his teeth. His patience once again starting to wear thin. He sighed.

"I know where you live in Hempstead Heath. Maybe I should pay your wife a visit, See if she can help me".

This got John's full attention. "leave her out of this"

Although sally and the twins weren't at home right now, he didn't want to let on.

"Only you can keep her out of this John, and those beautiful twins".

"You son of a bitch, leave them alone".

"All you have to do, is tell me what I want to know. My patience is running out; I will have to beat it out of you". Said Nick.

"Untie me, and try"

Nick chuckled.

"I know your background John. You like your mixed martial arts. I'm not a fool. I plan ahead. I have your phone here, you've spoken to Mike within the last couple days And you have a missed call from him. Maybe it's time to call him and say hello."

20

2100 HRS. NEWTON. IOWA.

I was driving through Newton Iowa, still on highway eighty. I pulled into a fuel station for fuel and snacks. As I went to pull back out onto the highway, my mobile phone rang, I pulled over to the side, so as not to block the exit.

"Hello John. I was going to try you again in a few hours. How's things with you?"

"Hello Mike" said the voice on the other end. It wasn't John's voice.

"Who is this"? I asked.

"You may call me, Nick. I have someone here who wants to say hello."

After a few seconds of silence he spoke again.

"It seems my guest is a bit shy right now. I'm sitting here with your friend John, trying to have a nice chat. But he isn't very forthcoming with the answers I want."

"Why should I believe anything you tell me"? I said.

"come on John say hello." Said Nick, on the other end. More silence. I heard Nick sigh, then I heard a thud, and a yell from John. "Fuck you" he shouted.

"Mike, I will get to the point. I have John here, I know where he lives. I know about his wife Sally, and the twins. You will cooperate or I pay them a visit."

"What do you want? you piece of shit"

"Now now, Mike. I've been nothing but nice. But I have things to do and my patience is running very low"

"what do you want? "I repeated.

"I want to know what you are up to. You are driving around America like you are on vacation. I know this has something to do with that case I took from you. If you are looking for it, you are wasting your time. It's gone."

"So, it was you. You got lucky. Who are you? Who do you work for?"

"Who I work for is of no concern to you, who I used to work for, well, John knows my old boss. Unfortunately, he had an accident and bled to death in his office." Nick chuckled.

I heard John shout "you son of a bitch. You will pay for that!"

"William paid for it, he found to much information. Unfortunate for him. So, you see Mike, I can't, and won't let any more information like that get out. That would be catastrophic for my new boss".

I thought I would go along with this, and see what he wanted.

"We have more evidence. You won't stop it this time. I'll be going to the authorities with this, and you'll be spending the rest of your days behind bars".

"If that evidence gets to the authorities. Your friend here will be spending the rest of his days lying next to William" said Nick.

"Leave him out if this. We can sort this out between ourselves."

"I want to see this evidence". Said Nick.

"It's in a safe place"

"You have 24 hours to show me this evidence, or your friend here will be sleeping with the bugs" said Nick.

He ended the call.

21

I called Stan and told him that I needed to get back to the UK. He wasn't happy about me leaving the situation over here. After I told him that John may be able to get a copy of the original evidence, he saw sense, and arranged flights for me.

Des Moines airport was the nearest international airport to where I was. I drove straight there to catch my flight to London. My flight was at three AM. I parked the truck in a long stay car park, got booked in, and found a comfy spot to chill in, I shut my eyes and tried and think about what I could do to help John. I would have to arrange to meet this Nick character and take him down somehow. First I needed to find out where he was holding John.

Stan said he would try and get location of John's phone. hopefully he would get that for me. My flight boarded. Once we are up to cruising height I tried and get some shut eye before the food came round. I managed to get some sleep before and after the food. Once we landed, I got myself through arrivals and went to get myself another hire car. Once that was sorted, I called Stan. He told me that he could get me to a place called Dorking, in Surrey. But he couldn't pin point the location.

It would take me less than an hour to get there, then put my plan in motion.

22

1100HRS SURREY, ENGLAND

Nick walked into the room and offered John water from the tin mug. John drank the water, then his mobile phone starts to ring.

"Ah, Mike. You have something for me?"

"I have what you want. We can meet somewhere and you can take a look" I said.

"I haven't got time to travel over there just to see if you are telling me the truth"

"You don't have to because I am back in the UK. We can meet today and get this done."

"I admire your dedication to your friend here, Mike. I will send you coordinates and you can head straight over."

"I will see you soon then" I said.

"I will be waiting"

The call ended and Nick smiled and turned to John and said..

 "You have a good friend there, John. It's a shame he has travelled all this way to save you, and he won't even get to see you. Now, if you'll excuse me, I have to get ready for his arrival."

"You got the better of him last time. Don't expect it to be so easy this time." Said John.

"Oh, I have a few surprises for him. And he won't see it coming".

He left the room, leaving John still tied to the chair. John knew he couldn't let Mike walk straight into whatever it was Nick had planned. He has to get free and help his friend. He struggled against his bonds, trying to work them loose. He eventually worked one wrist loose enough to take the pressure off. After waiting a few moments for the feeling to start coming back, he felt around his bonds and realised it was cable ties holding his wrists against the chair. He started working the cable tie against the back of the chair, he knew it wouldn't be easy to cut through a cable tie without a sharp instrument, but he had to try something to loosen them so he could get free. The chair was made from smooth metal and wood, so he had nothing rough to work the ties against. He finally decided that the only way he could free himself, was to dislocate one of his thumbs, so he could pull a hand free of the ties. He'd never done this before, but he has seen it done. He gritted his teeth hard, closed his mouth tight to stifle any noise he may make. Then he popped his thumb. He sat there for a few seconds catching his breath, then he forced his wrist free of the cable tie. Finally, he had some freedom. He pulled and stretched at the tie holding his other wrist and eventually worked his wrist out. He had cuts on his wrist and hands from the tie cutting into them, but he was free. He tried to see through the gap at the window, but couldn't see anything outside. He walked to the door and tried that. Locked, he knew it would be, but always worth a try. He put an ear against the door listening for any noise outside the room, but heard nothing. It was a normal timber framed wooden door. He knew he could break it open, but didn't want to alert Nick. He gripped the handle tight, hoping that he could force the door open and keep hold of it so it didn't fly open and make lots of noise. He gripped it tight then forced his shoulder against the door. It split the wood at the latch near the handle but didn't open. He shoulder barged it a second time and it popped open. He kept hold of the handle and waited a few moments for any noise or reaction from Nick. He heard nothing, so he slowly opened the door and looked out into the hallway. Another room opposite. He walked across the hallway to the other room and the window was boarded up in there too. He was upstairs, so he slowly walked towards the stairs and peered down them. Not seeing or hearing anything he went steadily down the stairs, stopping as he heard a noise. It came from outside; he couldn't work out exactly where it was coming from, but if it came from outside, then it was likely he was alone in the house. He carried on slowly down the stairs. Reaching the bottom he looked around, the house was pretty much empty of all furniture. He headed to the kitchen hoping to find something he could use as a weapon.

23

I turned down a track and pulled over to the side. I decided to walk to the coordinates so as not alert Nick to my arrival. I could see an old farm yard type place up ahead, so I stepped from the track into some trees and slowly worked my way towards the buildings up ahead. I wasn't one hundred percent sure I was in the right place, but I would find out soon enough. I kept on through the trees until I came to a waist high barbed wire fence. Looking around I could see small outhouse buildings, and a main house further into the farm yard. I turned right and followed the fence line slowly around to the back of the main house. The main house has boarded up windows so I couldn't tell if anyone was inside. I continued round the side of the house, still outside the fence line. As I got level with the back of the house I could see that the fence was no longer upright and there was more of an open area. If Nick wanted to plan an attack of some kind, this would probably be the area he did it. I moved cautiously, slowly heading towards the back door. I heard a noise in the area behind me, I looked round but saw nothing. I turned and made my way in the direction the noise had come from. Eventually I come to a small building about eight feet by ten feet, it looked like an outside toilet shed. I made my way slowly round the back, then a hand suddenly went over my mouth, and I was dragged into the building. A voice said "it's me, John."

Once John took his hand away I turned around to see him standing there, grinning.

"Am I glad to see you mate". He said.

24

John could find nothing useful in the kitchen area. He decided to make his way outside and see what he could find out there. He needed to try and find a way to keep Mike away from the house, because he didn't know what Nick planned for him. Surely he would want to see if what Mike has, was the real thing before doing anything stupid, but John wouldn't put anything past Nick. John made his way cautiously towards the back door. As he got to the door; he could see through a little gap in the boards covering the outside of the door. Seeing no one around, he tried the door and it wasn't locked, so he opened it slowly and took a cautious look outside. He made his way slowly out the door and walked towards a little out building at the back of the house. Once there he looked around for tools, or anything he could use to defend himself when the time came. All he found was a short length of rebar, about three quarter inch thick, and about two feet long, this would have to do. Just then from the corner of his eye he saw movement over by the fence line. He quickly went inside the little building and waited for a short while to see if he had been seen. He then peered round the door and saw Mike creeping towards the back of the house. He looked around for something small to get Mike's attention with. He found a small piece of log, that would do. He looked over to where his friend was, and he was heading for the back door.

John threw the piece of log in Mike's direction, then went to the corner of the small outhouse to watch. Mike made his way slowly over to the building John was hiding behind. As Mike went round the corner of the small building, John crept up behind him, wrapped his hand over his mouth and dragged him through the doorway. John then told Mike that it was him, then let him go.

25

"Sssshh," John mouthed whilst putting his finger to his lips. "He is out here somewhere, planning a welcome for you."

"Glad to see you are ok." I said.

"We need to stop this guy, Mike. He killed Will. He is planning to kill you too, and I guess I would be next".

"We need to split up and find him". I said.

"He doesn't know I've escaped. Maybe we can use that to our advantage. He will only be looking for you." Said John.

"Ok. Do you know what he's planning?"

"No, but I'm pretty sure its outside, because I didn't here him come back into the house."

"I think we need to clear these out buildings first. I'll check these two out back here. You check the bigger one on the other side of the house. Just watch your step mate. We don't know what he's up to." I said.

John went right, towards that side of the property, I went further into the farm yard, towards the two buildings behind the property. Some of the yard was overgrown with bushes, overgrown tree's, and rusty old farm equipment dotted around. I needed to find something to protect myself with. I walked slowly around the old machinery, keeping low as I went. The only thing I could find was a short length of chain, slightly thicker than you would find on a motorcycle, that would have to do. I kept moving slowly and carefully towards the first of the two buildings, keeping behind any type of cover I could find, which wasn't much. I got to the first of the two buildings, it was a standalone garage, big enough to fit maybe three cars inside and one more under a lean-to attached to the side of the building. I worked my way slowly inside, watching my step as I went. I didn't want to tread on something that would make enough noise to give away where I was. Once inside, I could see that there had been no cars in here for quite some time, just an empty space. Some of the corrugated roof sheets were hanging down inside. The walls had some good size cracks in them. I could see there was nothing of interest to me in here so I made my way back outside. My phone vibrated in my pocket. I pulled it out to see that John's phone was calling me. If I answered, it could give away where I was. The phone kept vibrating. He wasn't giving up. I answered the call, but said nothing.

"Mike, Mike, Mike," said Nick. I know you are out there, and I see you helped your friend get out too. I'm going to show you what a mistake that was. You should have left him where he was."

"I didn't get him out, he did that all by himself". I interrupted.

"He should have kept his nose out of this. Enjoy the fireworks".

As Nick ended the call, I realised what he was about to do. I ran outside and towards the other side of the property where John was looking, screaming as I went. Yelling at the top of my lungs.

"John get out. John get out." As I came around the corner of the property, the building ahead of me, that John was going to check, suddenly exploded with a massive bang. Bits of brick, stone, timber,smoke and dust went everywhere. I laid there against the wall of the main farm house, ears ringing and eyes starting to sting. Once the debris stopped falling, I looked over to what was left of the building. Only one corner was left standing, barely. I could see inside the part that was left, and no one would survive that blast. I shouted for John a few times, or at least I was trying to. I couldn't hear, or make out anything I was saying. I got to my feet and walked over to the wreckage. I knew I wouldn't find John alive, but I was hoping he hadn't been in the building at the time of the explosion. Having been in this situation before when I was in the military, I knew that was I was seeing, was remnants of body tissue. He had been inside. I sat down on a chunk of wall with tears welling up in my eyes. That only made them sting more. I shouldn't have got him involved. Sally and the girls will be devastated. I've lost a good friend, through no fault of his own. After a while my hearing started coming back. I stood, composed myself, took a few deep breaths, and went to find Nick.

"I'm coming for you" I shouted. Then my phone vibrated.

"Show yourself you piece of shit" I shouted, as I answered the phone.

"I was planning on ending you quickly Mike. But seeing you suffer is much more fun" said Nick.

"Fuck you. Show yourself, I will show you what it's like to suffer."

"I'm here Mike, you just gotta find me"

I looked around the area, there was no way to tell what else he'd done. I walked slowly round towards the front of the main house, watching where I stepped. I didn't want to set anything else off. I knew I would have to check the main house at some point, he wouldn't make this easy. I stopped and listened. All was quiet. I started walking again and heard a loud bang from inside the house, like a heavy object had been dropped. I walked to the front door and it was ajar. I slowly pushed my way in, watching every movement and step I made. I knew this could well be a trap, but I needed to get hold of him. I just needed to be careful and move slowly. Moving along the hallway, I heard a door slam. I couldn't rush through the house, that's what he wanted me to do. As I'm nearing the back of the house, I heard a metallic clang outside. I turned back the way I'd come and made my way back through the house. I got back to the front door and saw Nick running across the yard. I ran out the door and sprinted as fast as I could after him. He was quick, but I was quicker. It didn't take me long to catch up to him. He was heading for the main entrance to the yard. All caution had left me, I was only focused on catching him. I pushed as hard as I could to close the gap, then dived it his back. I missed his shoulders, so I wrapped my arms tightly around his waist and took him down. We hit the floor, scraping my elbows on the loose stones, I gritted my teeth and grappled to get up to his shoulders. He struggled as I tried to keep hold of him and punched between his shoulders a couple of times but he doesn't stop thrashing around. I rained down punches to any part of him I can get at but he managed to get his legs out from under me and started kicking out. We both ended up kicking out at each other, then I jump up to get a grip of him again, but he somehow managed to connect a kick to the side of my head, sending me back to the floor. He then jumped up and started running again, as I lay there for a second or two seeing stars. By the time I get back to my feet and set off after him, He has made it to a motorcycle. He manages to get out of my reach, but I give chase anyway. I couldn't let him get away. I kept running as hard as I could but he widened the gap. He got to the top end of the track and disappeared round the bend. I stopped running and bent down with my hands on my knees, trying to catch my breath. I realised my car should be just up ahead, so I ran up the track to where my car should be. It's was there where I left it. Something made me stop, something didn't feel right. I walk towards the car and when I was around ten feet away I bent down and looked underneath. As I suspected, he'd attached some kind of explosive device to the underneath of the car. It looked like a remote device; he was obviously going to set it off when he saw the car coming. I needed to get the car moving so he though it was being driven. I found a short piece of log, heavy enough to put a little pressure on the accelerator, but not too much. Hoping I'm right about the device, I got in the car and started it, no bang, so that's good. I turned the car around to point it towards the next bend. I've seen this done, not sure it will actually work, but worth a shot. I put the small log onto the accelerator pedal, put the car in gear and let the hand brake off. I gave the log a little press down for some pressure and the car slowly moved away. It seemed to be going the direction I needed it to, so I stood back and watched it roll up the track. It got to the bend, and before it went straight into the trees it exploded.

27

LOS ANGELES   SAME DAY

Stan sat in the office of his hillside mansion. He called for Danny to come join him. Danny arrived, shut the door and took a seat.

"What's going on boss". He said.

"We have a situation, Danny. As you know, Mike flew back to the UK yesterday. It turns out, that the guy who took that evidence from Mike, had his friend captive. His friend did manage to escape, only to be killed in an explosion. Mike himself nearly had the same fate, but luckily for him he spotted the device, but the other guy got away after blowing up Mike's car. We believe this man who calls himself Nick, is going to make his way over to the U.S. Mike is going to speak with his friend's family, then make his way back here. Once he is here, I want you to stick with him. We will house him here instead of the apartment, until this Nick character is dealt with. We need to watch his back. He is helping us with this problem, so we need to ensure he stays safe. Make sure your guys are up to speed, and have them tail you. I want your back up near you, at all times."

"You think this Nick guy knows Mike has help?"

"We are hoping he thinks Mike is dead. Then he will go straight to Rufus Longson, thinking he won't have any trouble."

"Don't you think, that if this Nick character had the evidence, he would have destroyed it by now?"

"Rufus will want to see the evidence for himself, before its destroyed. We don't believe he has it yet, so we need to get it first. Here are some photos of this Nick character, these are a few years old, but he shouldn't have changed that much. I have men at multiple airports looking out for him. We need to follow him and grab him before he gets to Rufus.

28

HAMPSTEAD HEATH. LONDON.

I called John's wife, Sally. I asked her to meet me at her house, as she was staying with her mother. After getting away from the farm in Surrey, I managed to hitch a lift back to London. My priority now, was to get to my apartment, get cleaned up, and meet with Sally. I wasn't looking forward to telling her that John was dead, but when I was in the military with John, he made me promise to be the one to break the news should the worst happen. I wasn't about to break that promise. The taxi I was in, pulled up at the house. As the taxi drove away I stood there for a few seconds trying to compose myself. I didn't know how I was going to do it. I took a few deep breaths as I walked to the front door. I didn't get chance to knock, as Sally opened the door as I approached.

"Hi" I said.

"I Haven't heard from John for a few days, Mike. Is he ok? Where is he?"

"Let's go inside Sally."

I followed her inside, shutting the front door behind me.

"Take a seat" I said.

"I don't want to take a seat, Mike. What's going on?"

"Sally, please sit down, I'll make you a cup of tea then we can talk"

"Mike, tell me what's going on". Her voice was raised slightly, her hands were shaking. She knew I hadn't come with good news.

"Oh my god, Mike. He's dead, isn't he? Oh, please don't tell me he's dead Mike. Please, no."

She was hysterical now. Her whole body was shaking. Tears were streaming down her face. She could barely get a breath in between the sobbing. The tears were starting to well up in my eyes again. I had to try and keep composed, for her sake. I managed to get her sat down. I sat next to her with my arms around her shoulders.

"I'm so sorry." I wasn't sure what to say next, so I just sat there until she was ready to talk. After a little while she asked what happened. She had to try a few times because she couldn't get the words out with all the sobbing.

"I'll make us a cup of tea, and we will talk" I said.

I pass her some tissues from the tissue box on the side, and went to the kitchen. I took her tea to her, and she waved it away. Placing the tea on a table next to her, I sat down. I thought about telling her a different story to what actually happened, But I couldn't do it. She deserved to know the truth. And that meant she needed to know he died helping me.

"John was helping me with something. He walked into a building and..."

I didn't know how to say the next bit ,However I put it, it was going to sound so violent, she wouldn't believe it.

"Just tell me Mike. Just tell me exactly what happened"

She wasn't shaking so much now, but still crying. I could see the anger building up now.

"John walked into a building and it exploded."

"What do you mean, it exploded? Buildings don't just

explode."

"He was in the building looking for someone, and walked into a trap."

She said nothing at this point.

"Sally, I was meant to be in that building when it

Exploded, it should have been me in there, not John."

"So why are you here right now and not John?" she said.

"A friend of John's was killed recently, and the guy who did that had John held captive"

I didn't get to finish that sentence because she jumped in.

"What the fuck do you mean ,captive. Why would he be held captive? What had you got him into?"

She looked at me with so much hatred, I was expecting her to start beating on me. "John was looking for his friend's killer, and when he found him, he ended up being held captive in an abandoned farm house in surrey." I said.

"And where were you when your best friend was being held in this farm house?" She said.

"I was in the U.S. I flew straight over here when I found out. He escaped from where he was being held, but ended up in that building, instead of me. I'm so sorry Sally. I wish I could swap places with him right now".

"Get out." She said, quietly.

"Sally, you shouldn't be alone right now. I can be there when you tell the girls if you like?" I said

"Oh, the girls. They are going to be heart broken. NO, I don't want you there. You've done enough already.

Because of you, my girls are going to grow up without a father."

"Sally" I said.

"No. Don't say another word. Just leave."

I pulled out a card and put it on her table. "This person will help with anything you need. Just call if you need anything."

"GO. GET OUT." she screamed.

29

I walked for an hour or so, trying to clear my head. The guilt I was feeling was like nothing I'd felt before. John got involved, trying to help me. I felt so angry with myself for involving him in this. I promised myself I would find Nick, and end him. He would finally pay for what he'd done. Stan had arranged flights for me, back to L.A. All I Wanted to do right now, was find Nick and bury him. It was highly likely he would go to L.A. and give the evidence case to this Rufus guy in San Francisco, now he thinks I'm dead. With Will, John and myself dead and buried he would be expecting no more trouble. Well he had a shock coming, he would be surprised next time he saw me. Once I got back to L.A I would be teaming up with Danny, and a team of us will be heading to where Rufus lived, ready to pounce when they meet. The flight was the usual for me, eat and sleep. Once we landed, I got through arrivals and was met by Danny.

"Hi" how's things?"

"Been better" I said. "Everything ready your end?"

"Yes, Iwill take you to Stan's place, then we will go

 through the plan."

"Ok. Good."

The journey was pretty quiet, A little small talk, but mainly silence. We eventually got to Stan's and he welcomed me with a big smile.

"Mike" he said. "so glad to see you are ok, considering what's happened."

"Thanks. I'll be happier when we end all of this. Most of all, when I put that bastard down."

"Your time will come, Mike. We will deal with this Rufus character, then we'll make sure you are the one who put's this Nick guy down. Come, we will go through what's next, over a stiff drink." Said Stan.

30

We spent the rest of the evening planning and drinking, then had a good meal. After being shown to my room, I showered and laid on the bed. That was where I stayed until morning. I woke up feeling tense. This was going to be a long day. I got myself sorted then went to find some coffee and food. Walking through the house, I was met by a staff member who asked me to follow her to a big room with a big table and chairs. She told me to take a seat, and she would be back with coffee and breakfast. She soon arrived with coffee and a big plate of food. I gave my thanks as she left, and dug in. After polishing off breakfast I made my way to Stan's office. He wasn't there, but Danny and another guy were there.

"Morning, Mike" said Danny. "how are you feeling

today?"

"Morning. I'm ready to get this over with."

"This is, Ryan" Danny said, pointing to the other guy in the room.

"Morning" I said, as we shook hands.

"Morning. I'm here to assist you and Danny with whatever you need."

"Thanks. Appreciate it."

"Stan asked me to get us some weapons, so they are in our vehicle. The other teams also have what they need." Said Ryan.

"Ok good."

"We will go in quietly, but whether it stays that way depends on Rufus and his men. If it turns noisy, we will be prepared. I understand that you have a military background. you will have a glock, and an M16 if needed. You ok with that?"

"Yes, that's fine." I said.

"We have eyes on the property. We will drive up to San Francisco, and head across to Berkeley when the sun goes down. Then wait for this Nick character to turn up. Once he in inside the property, we will go in. Slow and quiet to start with and see what happens. If it turns ugly, we go in hard and fast. Our priorities are, the evidence case, then take Nick and Rufus alive. They need to be alive or this is for nothing." Said Ryan.

"Hardly for nothing. He killed a friend of mine. He is going to pay."

"Yes, of course" said Ryan. "I didn't mean anything by it. I just meant that they will get away with it if they die in there"

"No worries mate" I said. They won't be getting away with anything"

31

The rest of that day, was spent travelling up to San Francisco. We all split up and did our own thing until the sun went down. We then met up and made our way across the Oakland Bay Bridge, and up into the Berkeley hills. We kept a couple of miles away from Rufus's property, waiting for confirmation that Nick had turned up. We sat in our vehicles, spread out around the perimeter of the property. We needed to cover all directions to and from the house. Once we got confirmation, we would go in from all sides, we needed to keep them from getting away. It had been a few years now, since I'd participated in any type of mission. The adrenalin was flowing now, these feelings bringing back memories from my time in the forces. We finally got word that Nick had just walked out of arrivals. And was now being tailed. We just had to wait for him to turn up. We thought about taking Nick when he pulled up in his vehicle, but we needed to keep this inside, out of the way of prying eyes. We only had to wait another half hour and we got word he was pulling in to the property. We waited for a couple of minutes, then got word to go in.

"All go. All go." Said a voice over the radio.

We drove towards the property. It only took a minute to get there. We parked up before getting too close, and went in on foot. We surrounded the building. Myself,

Danny, and Ryan, went to the front door. The other teams were placed at other entrance, and exit points. It was a big place so we needed to pin point the location of Nick and Rufus, and get there. We heard over the radio, that two of the teams could enter quietly at their locations, but the team posted at a side entrance would have to break in because they were locked out. They were told to hang tight unless it went noisy, then they could smash their way in. The other two teams and my team, let ourselves in quietly. We knew, Rufus had his security guys dotted around the property, but we didn't know exactly where they were. We needed to take them down fast and quiet as we came across them. One of the other teams had a contact, but dealt with it quietly. We were next to make contact with security. Two men were standing on a large balcony outside a set of patio doors. The doors were open, luckily for us. Myself and Ryan snuck across the room to the patio doors, whilst Danny covered us. Ryan and I let our rifles hang down on their slings. We looked at each other and nodded. We stepped silently towards the two security guys, only a couple of metres away. I went for the one on the right and Ryan took the guy on the left. We got behind them, then both, like lightening, we wrapped our arms around the two men, putting them in a sleeper hold, and put them out quietly. We heard loud whispers coming from outside the room. We brought our weapons up to the shoulder, waiting for whoever it was to enter the room. whoever it was continued past the room still talking. One was telling the other that security cameras had seen two men enter a back door to the property. We thought, previous to coming here, that we knew where all the cameras were. We'd fucked up. The men had been ordered to search the house quietly and bring whoever it was to the boss. We assumed that was Rufus. We alerted the two guys that had gone in through the back that they had been spotted. I had a feeling that this was about to go noisy. Not what we wanted.

32

We stepped cautiously out of the room. We had to find where Rufus and Nick were before it went noisy. That didn't happen. After clearing the next room, we heard gun fire coming from outside. The lads that were locked out, had company by the sound of it. We carried on through the house hearing shouts from different areas. Ryan was ahead of me and Danny was following behind. They told me they had orders to keep me safe. but I wasn't about to sit back and do nothing. I told them to do what they had to do. I could look after myself. They were having none of it. We rounded a bend in a long hallway and two men appeared from the other end. We put them down fast. Ryan took out one of them through the face, I took out the other just below the throat. We didn't take their weapons, but Ryan took on of their ear pieces so we could listen in to what they doing. We moved on through the house. We knew that a main office was at the rear of the property, so that's where we were headed. This was known to be his favourite spot to do business, so the chances of them being in there were high. We got to the end of the long hallway and took a right towards the rear of the house. We could still hear sporadic gun fire. We hadn't heard man down over the radio, so the other teams must be holding up ok. It occurred to me that the gunfire was in other areas of the house, not from the area we were heading to. The security guys were either waiting for us, or Rufus and Nick weren't where we thought they were, and could now be getting away. I voiced this to Danny and Ryan. They agreed that we could be wasting time all being in this part of the house. We decided to split up. I would carry on to the back office, Danny would go outside and come round the back of the office, and Ryan would search a different area. The guys disappeared and I carried on towards the office. I figured I couldn't be far away from it because I'd come quite a way through the house. I eventually made it to a pair of double doors. Solid oak by the looks of it. I radioed the guys and let them know I was there. Danny said he was still making his way to the rear of the office. Ryan still hadn't seen anything of Nick and Rufus. I could just about make out voices inside the office, muffled by the thick doors. Danny radioed me.

"I can see half of the office through the window, from where I am. I can see a red head sitting at a big desk, and two guys standing near him weapons in hand. I'd say there were more guys on the other side of the office, but can't be sure from here."

"Ok. We need to assume there are more guys in there. So, three guys you can see, we are probably looking at maybe four or five men in there. We need a distraction. We can assume, that red head is, Rufus. We need him alive."

"How do you want to proceed?" said Danny.

At this point, Ryan reappeared. Said he hadn't found them on the down stairs level. I explained the situation we were now in, with the office.

"I now have Ryan with me, so this is what we are going to do." I said.

I explained my plan and they agreed it was the best way to deal with this. I counted down. three.... two.... one....

Danny let loose with a barrage of gun fire through the back-office window, aiming at the guys stood near Rufus. As soon as he started firing, I set of some explosives we had stuck to the door. The doors came of the hinges in bits. The firing had stopped momentarily as the area filled with smoke. Ryan made his way cautiously through what was left of the door frame. I followed closely behind. Ryan took out a guy sitting stunned on the floor. Nobody else seemed to be moving. Danny climbed in through the window frame and spotted Rufus lying on the floor behind his desk. He was covered in dust and debris. I went over and grabbed him and helped him up into his chair. he wasn't sure what was going on, but was unhurt so that was good news. I checked the bodies on the floor, and Nick was not among them.

33

I radioed the other teams and told them to look out for Nick. I was really pissed off that he was not there. Our main objective was to get Rufus. We had done that. Now we needed to find this evidence and make use of it. I still needed to find Nick before he disappeared Again. Two men from one of our teams turned up to help Ryan find the suitcase, and keep an eye on Rufus. We didn't want him running off too. Myself and Danny set off to find Nick. It was making my blood boil thinking he might get away again. We went outside, there were a few bodies lying around from the firefight. We checked them all, making sure none of them were Nick. None were, so we moved on. We searched everywhere inside the perimeter wall; he was nowhere to be seen. We went back inside the house. Maybe Rufus can give us his whereabouts. When we arrived back at the office, one of our guys was arguing with Rufus. He wouldn't tell them what they wanted to know. I was more concerned about Nick's whereabouts. They had the guy that Stan wanted, it was up to them to find the missing evidence. All I wanted to do now, was get hold of Nick and make him pay for what he'd done. I broke up the argument and asked Rufus where Nick was. He said he doesn't know. I saw red and grabbed him by the throat.

"Listen to me. You know where he is, and you are going to tell me."

"I don't know where he is. He was here before you showed up. He left when we saw two of your men on camera," said Rufus.

"Where is he headed?" I asked.

"I don't know. I swear."

I thought it was time to call Stan. He needed to know we had his man. And I had a question for him.

"Hello, Mike."

"Stan, we have Rufus. The evidence seems to have disappeared with Nick. I have a question. "If the tracker that was in with the evidence, was lost as it got to L.A. why are we still chasing it? And why would Nick still be running around with it?"

"We believe that the evidence was switched to a different case. Why the original one was sent over to the states is anyone's guess. We didn't realise this until you told me what happened in the U.K.," said Stan.

"So, he sent an empty case with a tracker in it, overseas, to throw us off the scent. That didn't really work, with the GPS tracker not working."

"Well, he has the new one and we need to get it back. Can you get more men on this Stan?"

"Yes, of course. I will get more guys on this right away."

"Do we let Rufus go? Maybe Nick will be back. He obviously has what Rufus wants so he will be looking for a window of opportunity to get it to him." I said.

"I agree. He will want to make contact with him again. leave him there, the guys you have there can watch the house. If Rufus goes out anywhere, they follow. They don't let him out of their sight. I will get the men here, looking for any trace of Nick." Stan said.

"Ok. As soon as Nick is found, I want to know about it."

"Rest assured, Mike. You will be the first to know."

34

After looking everywhere for Nick, we went to our vehicles. Myself, Ryan, and Danny, left the property and had a drive round the area. The rest of our guys kept an eye on the property, to watch Rufus in case he decided to leave the house, or Nick turned up again. We had no luck finding him on our drive around. It was now in the early hours of the morning, so we decided to call it a night. We drove back into San Francisco and went back to our hotel rooms to try and get a few hours' sleep. I thought about calling Sally, but I wasn't expecting a good response and it had already been a long day.

I woke around six AM. Showered, then went to find some breakfast. I settled for a McDonald's. It had been a while since I'd had one, and I like their coffee. After eating, I went for a walk. I had no idea where Nick would be, but I could only hope that him and Rufus met up soon. I knew Stan wouldn't give up until we had him and the evidence back. I wouldn't either. I received a call from, Danny.

"Mike, Rufus has just left the house. The guys are on his tail. He's heading towards San Pablo, and the Richmond bridge."

"Ok. I'm on my way back, we'll take the car and head out. He's going to avoid the city. We need to be out there ready to intercept."

I arrived back at the hotel and we got straight in the car and left. We just needed to keep on the move for when we got confirmation, he had been found. We got word that Rufus was heading back down into the city. He was on the west side. I told Danny to head over in that direction. The guys told us he was driving a white jag 4x4. And gave us the registration. Ryan was all smiles in the back seat.

"What are you so cheery about?"

"I'm looking forward to grabbing these two." He said.

"Remember. Nick is mine." I said.

"I know, I know. He's been giving us the run around. Be good to stop him."

"That it will, mate. That it will." I said.

35

Whilst we were driving around, I wondered where Rufus's wife Carol was, in all of this. There was no sign of her at the house. No one had heard from her. I mentioned this to the guys.

"Stan may be able to find out." Said Danny. I decided to called Stan right then.

"Hi Mike."

"Hi. Can you find Carol Longson and make sure she is, ok?"

"Yes. Will do. Do you think something's happened?"

"I don't know. There was no sign of her at the house last night. Just be good to check on her."

"I will get right on it. I'll get back to you when I know something."

"Thanks. We are following Rufus right now. We are hoping he is meeting up with Nick. Will keep you informed."

"Ok. I'll be in touch" said Stan.

The call ended. I hoped he would find carol safe and well. I just didn't have a good feeling about it. The fact that Rufus knew about the evidence, makes me wonder if he'd done something to keep his wife quiet. Or did he just plan to intercept the evidence without her knowing, and hope this problem just went away. Either way was not good for Carol. We needed to get it back so she could do what she needed to do. Then that piece of shit will spend the rest of his days behind bars. As for Nick, well. We all know what I want to do with him. After keeping in touch with our other teams, we finally caught up with Rufus. He was heading down the west side of the city on highway one. We were eight vehicles behind him, one of our team cars was four vehicles behind. The other team vehicle was keeping near but awaiting instructions. All we could do right now, was follow and see where he went. Between the three of our vehicles we switched positions sporadically. We didn't want to keep the same vehicles in the same positions, because it may become obvious to him that he was being followed. My adrenalin was slowly starting to kick in. I just wanted to grab these guys and hope he has the evidence, then we could be done with this. We followed Rufus to a place called, Pedro Point Headlands. Highway one went through these hills on the west side. He was heading for the parking lot at Devil's slide trail. We couldn't follow him to the parking lot because there weren't many vehicles around and we would stand out like a sore thumb. Danny dropped me and Ryan off, and we ran up ahead on foot. Guys from the other vehicles were out on foot too. All we could do was confirm his vehicle was in the parking lot and go look for him. We soon got to the parking lot area; his car was nowhere to be seen. The parking lot only had spaces for seven or eight vehicles. We went further up the road and noticed a dirt track running parallel with the road we were on, but went behind bushes and trees. We couldn't see along the track from where we were standing, so we needed to move up the track. We set of running, two more of our team members were now with us. We continued for a few hundred metres then came across a little hut. Probably fifteen feet by twelve feet. It only had one window, which was boarded up. As we got closer, we noticed the back of a white vehicle tucked around the side of the hut. We'd found him. We split up and surrounded the little hut. It was definitely his vehicle. No other vehicles were here. We crept towards the hut hoping to hear some voices. That's exactly what we heard, but it wasn't two male voices we heard. One was female.

36

We continued to listen; we could only hear muffled words. There was no arguing, just chit chat. I'm thinking he has Carol in there. Why? I don't know, but I'm sure it's her. I tell the guys to get back and keep out of sight. If that is Carol inside, we can go in and get her out without him knowing. We needed to wait until Rufus left. It was around fifteen minutes later when he finally left. He came out alone, and locked the door. Nick definitely was not in there. We kept out of site until he left. Once he had driven away, I instructed one of our teams to tail him. We waited for five minutes then I approached the hut and tried the door, it wouldn't take much to get it open. With Ryan watching my back, I took a step back and kicked hard at the door. It splintered but didn't come open. I heard a muffled scream from inside. I stepped back and kicked through the door a second time. It flew open hanging from one hinge. I followed it in, with Ryan following behind. The place was pretty empty apart from a camp bed that Carol was now sat on and a bucket for her toilet. A small wooden table was next to the bed for her food and water. Carol was chained to the wall next to the bed, the chain just long enough for her to reach the bucket, and bed. The rest of the hut was empty. I walked slowly over to her.

"I'm not going to hurt you. We are here to help. I'm going to take the cloth from your mouth." I said.

I slowly undid the cloth tied around the back of her head. She flinched as I did so. I reminded her we weren't there to hurt her. I removed it and threw it aside.

"Hi. We are here to help. We know about the evidence you found against your husband. We didn't know he was keeping you here like this. How long have you been in here?" I said.

"Couple of weeks I think" said Carol.

"Ok. Let's see if we can get these chains off. Then we can talk."

Between myself and Ryan, we managed to break the chains and free her arms. Ryan handed her a bottle of water. She took a sip and put the bottle on the table.

"How did you know where to find me?"

"We've been following Rufus for a while. Are you aware of a man called, Nick? We believe he has the evidence you found, but has not yet handed it over to Rufus. We need to get it back before he sees it, and destroys it."

"Rufus told me that I'm to stay put until he has sorted this out. What he means by that, I don't know. He comes here or sends one of his guys two or three times

103

a day to bring food and water. I'm afraid what he is going to do to me when he's dealt with all of this."

"He won't get near you now. I can promise you that." I said.

"I have nowhere to go. All of my belongings are at the house."

"you don't need to worry about that. We will keep you somewhere safe until this is all over."

37

I called Stan to arrange for Carol to stay there until this was all sorted.

"I can take care of that, but I would like you to personally bring her back here. The guys are keeping an eye out for Nick, so don't worry about him getting away again. We will get you back up there asap."

"Ok, but I do need to be back here to deal with him."

"We'll make it happen."

The call ended. We were going to have to drive back to L.A. Carol had nothing with her, just the clothes she had on. Danny turned up and we all got in his vehicle. Once we had got fuel and food supplies for the journey, we set off. It was going to be late when we got back. We would get Carol settled, then the following day we could head back up to San Francisco. It wasn't long before Carol was sleeping, she probably hadn't slept much, chained up like she was. She was safe now, we just needed to concentrate on finishing this so we could get back to our lives. It was three hours into the journey when Carol needed to stop for the toilet. We stopped at the next opportunity and all stretched our legs whilst Carol sorted herself out.

Apart from the toilet, we never let her out of our sight. A truck pulled into the service station, but didn't go to the fuel pumps. All blacked out window's, shiny wheels. It went round the back of the shop area. It always amazed me, why people spent all that money jazzing up their vehicles. Maybe I was just getting old. Danny finished fuelling our vehicle and went into the shop to pay, and get some snacks. Carol finally finished and walked back to our vehicle. I could tell she'd tried to clean herself up a bit. We all got in and set off again.

38

A man was sitting in his vehicle, talking on his phone.

"I'm still tailing them. They stopped for fuel and have just left again."

"Ok. Don't lose them. We need to know where they are taking her. When they get to where they are going, let me know."

"Will do." Said the man.

The call ended and the man started up his truck and pulled out of the fuel station. Rufus knew they would find Carol, but he didn't think it would take them this long. He had destroyed the evidence the day he had received it. His men had found the tracker and stuck it to someone else's luggage at the airport. They had put a tiny device on it to block the signal, timed to block it once it landed in L.A. He was pleased with himself for pulling this off. Of course, knowing these tech heads as he did, helped. He now needed to know who else was involved with all of this, then he could shut them all up. His plan then, was to make his wife Carol's death look accidental then claim all the finances she has, for himself. He already got a load of money from her dad's death, now he wanted the rest. He knew he was greedy, but he didn't care. His plan to have, William and John killed had gone how he had expected.

He hadn't counted on Mike being such a pain in the arse. He'd done his homework on John, and knew he could be a difficult target. he was first on the list, but William ended up in the wrong place at the right time, so he got his first. Rufus thought, with those two out of the way he could wrap this up quickly. He was wrong. He couldn't find anything on Mike, but he now knew he wouldn't be easy to get rid of. He had his man following him. and his cousin Nick, was safe and sound in the house. He was well hidden when Mike and his goons had barged in.

"How's the road trip going so far?" said Nick as he walked into Rufus's office.

"Our man is on their tail. He won't let them out of his sight."

"I'm telling you Rufus; we should have sent more men to follow them. This Mike fella is more ruthless than we gave him credit for. And he clearly has well connected friends."

"Don't worry about him. Once we know who his new friends are, we will deal with them hard and fast. They won't see it coming. You worry too much."

"I've been up close and personal with that man. He is not going to give up. I killed his friend; he won't let that go. I was lucky to get away from him when I did. He won't let me get away again."

"He won't get near you next time. We will take him and his friends out, the way you took out his friend John."

"I don't know how you plan to do that." Said Nick.

"You let me worry about that. You just need to be ready to light up their world. They will get what's coming. I promise you that."

39

I could have sworn twice now, that I'd seen that blacked out truck from the services, a way behind us. It must be a popular way to do up trucks these days. I was getting tired; we'd taken it in turns to drive. We had stopped a couple of times to stretch our legs and get coffee. We pulled up outside Stan's place, and he came out to greet us.

"Good to see you all back in one piece. We need a little chat, once we have Mrs Longson here, settled."

Stan asked one of his female staff members to see Carol to a room that would be hers until this was over. I followed Stan to his office. Once in, he shut the door and offered me a drink. I sat down on one of the comfy seats as Stan brought my drink over. He sat down opposite me.

"So, apart from finding and rescuing Carol. Did anything useful come out of your trip?"

"Well we didn't get hold of the evidence. Nick got away AGAIN. Rufus was pretty much useless to us, well apart from leading us to Carol. So, no. Not really."

"We've found out something interesting. It turns out that Nick and Rufus are cousins."

"You've got to be shitting me?" I said.

"Nope. Nick's mother is a sister to Rufus's dad. We only found this out yesterday. Turns out he went to work for William Selmonns after Rufus found out there was a possibility of some evidence about his wrong doing. Nick had been transporting stuff for Rufus prior to that."

"So, Rufus managed to get him the job with William, so he could grab the evidence before it got to his wife. He must have had an idea that his wife was looking for proof."

"It looks like it. We don't know how he got the job so quick. Rufus obviously pulled some strings."

"Slimy bastard. They've been on top of this from the start." I said.

"I guess that, Nick had to hand it over to you so it would show that he did his part, he confirmed he'd handed it over with William, then took it back. We will finish this, Mike. Carol is safe, we know where Rufus is. And I bet Nick isn't far away."

"We need to get back up to San Francisco, soon as. I'm not letting him get away again."

"Like I told you. Our guys are on it. You need to rest for a day or two here. Refresh, then we can get back up there and deal with this. Hopefully by then we will have Nick pinned, and we can go get him. We need to assume the evidence has been destroyed already.

We've been looking into William's investigation business, trying to figure out if we can get hold of another set of that evidence. My guys are on it, if there is more to be had, they will find it." Said Stan.

"Two days, then we go back up there."

"Two days."

We ended our conversation. Said our goodnights, then went to grab some sleep.

40

Rufus sat at his office desk talking to Nick who was sitting opposite him. Their conversation was interrupted by the phone ringing.

"Hello." Said Rufus.

"Boss. I followed them to a place called Baldwin Hill. Calver City. L.A. I couldn't get close enough to follow to a property, what do you want me to do?"

"Just stay in the area, I will get some more men over to you. Keep an eye out for them leaving the area again. When the guys get with you, you need to find that property. We need to get Carol back by any means necessary." Rufus ended the call.

"Our man knows where they are hiding out. We need to send him some guys to help get Carol back, then we can end them."

"I don't know why you won't just end her at the same time. She is there, they are all together. Perfect opportunity." Said Nick.

"I've already told you. I need to make her death look accidental. And I don't mean, blown to pieces. You know what she is worth to me".

"You mean, what she is worth to you dead. You only married her for the money. You got a lot when her dad died. We have enough business going on, you don't need her money."

"Correct, I don't need her money. I want it! Her dad's money has made us rich. Her money will top that off nicely. We've made a lot of money from the properties we've bought and sold, with that money he left. She has served her purpose. We now know where they are. We get her back, finish them, and get rid of her. Then I will be happy." Said Rufus.

"Let's hope this all goes as simple as you make it sound."

41

I went to get some breakfast. A full-on feast. The cooks here really know how to put on a spread. Once I'd finished, I took my coffee out on to the back patio and sat there soaking up the sun. It wasn't long before Danny came out and joined me.

"Morning, Mike"

"Morning mate."

"So, Stan has told you to stay put for a day or two. How do you feel about that?"

"To be honest, it makes sense to recharge while I can. We don't know where Nick is. Hopefully keeping away from there may entice him to turn up again. I just want to get this over with so I can get back home and sort some things out." I said.

"I guess you have a few loose ends to tie up hay"

"You could say that. First I need to see John's wife and daughters and make sure they are taken care of. Then I need to sort myself out. I don't know what I'll do after this. This secret business is proving to be more hassle than it's worth, to be honest."

"You could always come back over here and work with us. I'm sure Stan would be happy to have you on the team."

"And spend my days chasing people, and getting shot at. No thanks. Been there done that. It's time for a change."

"Well, Think about it Mike. We could do with a guy like you around here. You know your stuff. You get stuck in. You'd be a good team player."

"Thanks. But I don't know what my future holds right now. I just know I plan to finish this before I do anything else." I said.

"I guess you have a lot to be down about right now. But this will all work out, Mike. And then you can relax and think about what it is you want out of life."

"I'd like my friends back mate. I've lost friends before, but John was like a brother to me. This will always haunt me."

"I wish there was something I could do to help"

"Just help me end this. That's all I need help with right now." I said.

"We will end this together"

I stood up and put my hand on Danny's shoulder.

"You're a good one Danny don't change. I'm going for a walk. Be back soon."

I walked out onto the main road. Turned right, and just walked. I didn't know this area so I stuck to the main route. I walked for about twenty minutes, then came up to a little pull in off the road. There were two vehicles parked there, a little two-seater sports car, and a blacked out pickup truck. This sent my senses tingling; I was Seeing a lot of these lately. I walked towards it. I couldn't see anyone inside, so I walked up to it and looked inside. Apart from a scrunched-up empty cigarette packet on the passenger seat and a couple of half full bottles of water, there was nothing out of the ordinary. I guess everyone has the same taste when it comes to trucks. I walked away and continued down the hill.

42

The truck owner walked out from behind some bushes. That was a close one, he thought to himself. He'd been trying to find the property where Carol was being kept. Once he'd found the place, he walked back to where his truck was parked. He was about to walk out from the trail he was on, when he saw a guy walking over to his truck. He watched the man look over his truck and then just walk away. The man got back to his truck, pulled out of the parking area, and drove away. A little way down the road he passed the man walking down the hill. There was something about that man, familiar looking. Could be from the property where Carol was. The man had photos of Mike and Danny and he looked similar to one of them, but he didn't get a good look at him to be sure. He pulled up at the spot he'd been parked overnight. Just a little clearing off the main road, out of sight. He could keep an eye on the road from that spot. He called Rufus. "Boss, I found the house where Carol is being held."

"Excellent. Stay where you are until our guys get there. But keep an eye on things if anyone leaves, let me know." Said Rufus.

"One of the guys is out having a walk right now. I think it may be Mike, but didn't get a proper look at him."

"Was he alone?"

"Yes. He was walking down the hill not far from where I am now."

"Hold on a minute" said Rufus.

Rufus had a quick chat with Nick in the background, then came back on the line.

"Can you grab him?"

"You want me to grab him? Now?"

"Can you do it or not?"

"Sure. Yes boss."

"Ok. If you see him, grab him. Be careful. He can handle himself."

"No problem boss. I will deal with him." Said the man.

"Good man. Do it quick. Let me know when you have him. And keep him out of the way."

"Will do boss."

The call ended. It was time to earn himself a bonus. He pulled out of the spot he was in, and drove back up the hill.

43

I was walking back up the hill to go back to Stan's place, when that blacked out truck passed me again. That's twice now since I saw it parked earlier. It was headed back up the hill from where it came from. I kept walking, my mind was filled with how I was going to talk to sally when I got back to the U.K. It wouldn't be easy, but I couldn't leave things the way they were. I knew her and the twins would be fine financially, John always made sure, of that. But living without him, was going to take a lot of getting used to. For me also. I got a little further up the hill when I saw the truck pulled to the side of the road, with a flat tyre. There was a man changing the wheel, he looked like he was struggling with it. As I got closer, he saw me, and caught my eye.

"Hey man. Could you help me please?"

I walked towards him as he was trying to get the truck jacked up. He looked like an average bloke. Jeans. T shirt. Boots. And a baseball cap, low over his eyes.

"How can I help?" I asked.

"Ah man, so glad you came along. I can't get this truck jacked up. It's a new truck and I haven't used this jack yet. It just won't play ball." He seemed genuine, and friendly enough.

"Where are you going. You've been up and down this road a couple of times. You lost?" I said.

"No, the man said with a chuckle. A friend of mine lives around here and it's the first time I've visited him. I couldn't find his place, so I called him and he directed me. Now this damn tyre decided to go flat."

"Well that's frustrating. Let's have a look." I said.

"Thanks man. You're a life saver. I've been planning on coming out here for a while now. When I finally get chance to visit, it's just been one of those days."

"We'll get you on your way in no time. Where have you travelled from?"

"Travelled down from San Francisco yesterday. Was going to fly down, but wanted to test out the truck."

"This blacked out theme. Seems quite popular."

"Yes sir. It's a good way to make the truck look good without spending too much."

"Makes sense, I guess. Ok. Let's get this wheel changed."

We both set about getting the wheel changed, then Got the truck back on its wheels.

"Where do you want this wheel putting" I said as I picked up the wheel with the flat tyre.

"Just chuck it in the back there."

As I placed the wheel in the back of the truck, I something touch my ribs.

"Step around to the side of the truck real slow mister. Don't make any sudden movements or I will shoot you."

"Hey man. You don't need to do this. I have money, just take it." I said.

"I don't need your money. Once my boss see's that I have you. I will get a generous bonus."

"Your boss? Who is y..........?

My world went dark at that point.

44

"Boss. I have him. He is tied up in the back of my truck. Knocked out for now."

"Excellent. You can expect a good bonus for this. I will soon send you an address. You are to take him to that address; there you will meet the guys I sent to help you. You will hold Mike at that address. Until my cousin arrives. Is that clear?" said Rufus.

"Loud and clear boss"

"Good man"

The call ended. After waiting for a good twenty minutes, the man's phone pinged. It was the address from Rufus. Some place in the franklin canyon in the Hollywood hills. The GPS told him it was just under twelve kilometres away. This shouldn't take too long. He thought. He pulled out from his little hiding spot, and drove off towards his destination.

 Back in San Francisco. Rufus was celebrating with a whisky, even though it was still early in the day.

"This is going to work out perfect. He will tell us what we need to know. And you can finish him."

"It won't be a quick death like his friend. He will suffer. We will see just how tough he really is." Said Nick.

"You have everything ready?" asked Rufus.

"I managed to get a flight later on today. By this evening he will be squealing like a pig. Rufus smiled it this.

"Make sure you record it. I would like to see him suffer. Wish I could be there. But I have things to deal with this end."

"I will record every moment. Once he is dealt with, we can get Carol back and end this." Said Nick.

"Yes. We will be wealthier, and ready to move our other projects forward."

"You are a greedy man Rufus." Nick said, smiling.

"Yes. Yes I am." Rufus laughed hard at this. The two of them chinked glasses and toasted to the future.

45

Danny walked through the house and knocked on Stan's office door.

"Come in."

"Stan, we may have a problem." Said Danny.

"What kind of problem?"

"Mike went out for a walk a few hours ago, he hasn't returned."

"What. Where did he go." Said Stan.

"He just said he was going for a walk and would be back soon."

"How long ago was this?"

"Three hours, ish."

"Have you tried his phone?"

"A few times, its off."

Stan tried ringing Mike; the phone was off.

"Shit. Ok, grab a couple of guys and have a drive round, see if you can find him."

"OK."

"And keep in contact with me. I want to know what's going on." said Stan.

Danny gathered up a couple of the guys and set off to look for Mike. They drove around for some time. Up and down little streets. Working their way slowly away from the property.

Just under 12 kilometres away. I came round on the back seat of a vehicle. It took me a few seconds to realise where I was. I was tied up in the back of the blacked-out truck. I knew that because the driver was still sat in his seat, smoking a cigarette. It was the guy who I had helped change a wheel.

"What is all this?" I asked.

 He turned round in his seat and smiled.

"Ah hello sleepy head. This is me getting a good bonus. Thanks to you walking by, I will be able to pay for extras on this beauty."

"You did this to pay for extras for your truck?"

"No no. I did this to please my boss. He was over the moon when I told him I had you tied up in my truck. He told me to expect a good bonus for it. He's a good boss."

"Yeah, sounds like a real gent." I said, sarcastically.

"Who is this boss of yours?"

"You will find out soon enough. Once my friends get here, you will be answering questions, not asking them."

I wasn't sure who he worked for, but I had a bad feeling this was something to do with Rufus. If this was the case, I needed to get out of here before his mates turned up.

"How about you untie me. I'll pay you double the bonus you were going to get and you can just say, I got the jump on you and ran away."

"I don't think so." The man said, laughing.

"You think you could get the jump on me. I must have hit you hard. Anyway, here come my friends."

I could hear a vehicle approaching. It pulled up just past where we were parked. The man got out of the truck. I heard voices talking, but couldn't make out what they we're saying. He then reappeared and opened my door. Two other guys dragged me out roughly, and dropped me to the floor. I was kicked three or four times before the truck driver intervened. He told the other guys that the boss wanted me un harmed. They then picked me back up and frog marched me into an old property that looked like it hadn't been lived in for a while. They took me down into a basement. And tied my hands to a post in the middle of the room. I was sat on the floor, hands tied behind my back. I thought I was going to be there for a while. I got as comfortable as I could and just waited for whatever would happen next.

46

I had been left in the basement for a few hours. No one had offered me food or water. I started to prepare myself mentally for what may come. They clearly didn't give a shit about my wellbeing. Not one person had checked on me, made sure I was ok. I was just trying to keep myself as comfortable as I possibly could. It wasn't much longer when the door opened and who should walk in, Nick. I couldn't believe it. He had a big smirk on his face. Whatever he was planning, he was looking forward to it. I tried my best to keep poker faced, but I was absolutely seething with anger. I just wanted to rip his throat out, and wipe that smug look off his face.

"Well well well. The almighty Mike isn't looking so mighty now. I've been dreaming of ways to make you suffer, and believe me, you are going to suffer." Said Nick.

"Screw you. Untie me and take me on like a man."

"Now now, Mike. Don't be like that. We are going to be spending some quality time together. Unlike your friend John, you won't be so fortunate as to die quickly."

"Fuck you." I said.

Nick laughed and left the room. I needed to find a way out of this. I had no doubt about his intentions. I started to work one part of my bonds against the concrete column hoping to wear through them. Feeling the smoothness of the post, I knew it would take some time to start to wear the rope out. Hopefully it would eventually wear through enough for me to loosen it and get free. after a little while Nick reappeared. He was carrying a small plastic tool box. He still had that stupid smirk on his face. I stopped moving my hands, and hoped that he didn't notice any marks or anything to give away what I was doing.

"Mike, Mike, Mike, where do I start. I've been thinking about how to make you suffer, but now I'm here. I don't know where to start."

"You can start by telling me what you want"

"Well, Mike. Firstly, I would like to know how many men are in that hillside mansion you are keeping Carol in?"

"I'm sure you will find that out soon enough. Or maybe you won't." I said.

"You are soon going to have more dead friends, Mike. Co-operating may spare some of them."

"You aren't getting a word of help from me. Trying to get Carol out of there, will be suicide. So please feel free to try."

"We will try. And we will succeed. And once we have Carol back. Your friends will be obliterated."

"I'm done talking. Just get on with it." I said.

"Tough guy? ok, if that's what you want."

He picked up his little tool box and sat it on an old wooden bench attached to one of the walls. He pulled out a few items. A small hacksaw. Screwdrivers. Stanley knife. What looked like a handful of nails. Then he smiled and pulled out what he was looking for. He turned to look at me and said.

"I'm going to enjoy this"

47

Stan walked down to his extensive basement. It housed thousands of bottles of wine. A library full of rare, and old books. And a small room full of his favourite rum, whisky, and brandy. Through to the back of the basement was a steel door with a keypad entry system. He typed in his seven-digit security code, then the system asked him to put his finger on the scanner. Once the system had excepted his ID, it unlocked and he walked in, Shutting the fireproof sealed door behind him.

"Billy" he shouted.

Billy was a 37-year-old. He looked like an overweight surfer dude, with his long blonde hair, and he had an unhealthy obsession with cheeto's.

"Be there in a minute boss."

Stan had a look at the screens that were arranged around Billy's work station. There was CCTV for the whole property. CCTV for the surrounding perimeter fence line. And Stan had camera's dotted around the surrounding area. Watching the roads in and out. They could see pretty much up to nearly five miles from the property.

132

"What can I do for you, boss?" said Billy as he walked back in the room. He had his own little suite in the adjoining room. Fully kitted out, and he lived there.

"Can you check on Mike's last known position?"

"Sure, thing boss."

Billy sat at his work station, it was a semi-circular table, covered with laptop's, and notebooks, and papers of some kind. Stan never questioned Billy about the way he kept his work space. Billy knew where everything was, and he always did what Stan asked of him, whether he agreed with it or not. This was his domain. He kept it the way he liked it. On the wall in front of where Billy sat were screens and computer monitors. Eight in total. Some were split screens for cameras. And the rest were for whatever else Billy did in there. Stan respected Billy's space. He tapped some key's and brought up some camera feeds from earlier on in the day.

"We should start from early-ish this morning, say eight o'clock." Said Stan.

"No problem"

He brought up the camera feeds and they started to look through them slowly, looking for the first signs of, Mike. It wasn't long before he appeared.

"Ok, there he is."

"Quarter past eight. Just forward it slowly."

Billy played the feed, and they watched Mike walk down the hill away from the property. Another couple of minutes and they watched Mike walk over to a blacked-out truck and look inside. After a few seconds, he walked away and carried on down the hill. Billy tapped the forward key again to follow Mike, then Stan stopped him.

"Hold on. Go back to where Mike was looking in that truck."

Billy wound it back to that part of the camera feed.

"There." Said Stan. "let it play at normal speed."

Billy pressed play and they watched it back again at normal speed.

"There stop. This guy here, he walked out of the bushes as soon as Mike walked away."

"Who is he?" Billy asked.

"No idea" Keep on him. See what he's up to.

48

As Nick turned round to face me, he was holding a small lump hammer. I tried my best not to look at it, but it was hard not to.

"Guys" shouted Nick.

Two big fella's walk in.

"I need him standing, legs bound too."

The two guys walked over to me. One walked behind and started to slide my arm bindings up the post and one of them help to lift me into a standing position. Once I was standing, I kicked out at the guy in front of me, hitting him in his ribs. He took it well, then punched me hard in the face. He looked round at Nick and said he was sorry. They'd obviously been told that Nick was to do all of the physical stuff.

"He deserved that, don't worry about it. Get his legs tied."

They tied my legs tight; I was in a standing position against the post I couldn't sit down or relax now. This was going to be unpleasant by itself. Once they had me how they wanted me, the two big guys left, shutting the door behind them.

Nick walked over to me, he bent down and started taking my boots off. I tried to struggle and make it difficult for him, but my legs were tied too tight.

"No point struggling, Mike. I told you I was going to make you suffer, and that is what's going to happen."

He took off my boots, then he walked over to the wooden bench and picked up the lump hammer. This was it; I was going to have to take some serious pain now.

"It's time Mikey boy. Time to have some fun. Feel free to make as much noise as you like. No one will hear your screams."

"You won't hear them either."

"Oh, so brave Mike. Let's see shall we."

He walked over to me. Looked me in the eye and just stared for a few seconds. I spat in his face. He didn't flinch. He never did anything for a few seconds, then he wiped his face with the back of his sleeve. He bent down, lifted the hammer, and smashed it down hard onto my left big toe. I let out an almighty yelp. It made my eyes water. It hurt like fuck. I tried to take it with gritted teeth but it was excruciating.

49

Stan and Billy, continued to watch the man with the truck. He walked out from the bushes, walked back to his truck, started it and drove away back down the hill. They continued to watch as the truck drove passed Mike.

"Forward it again, Billy."

Billy skipped forward slowly. They continued to watch. Eventually they saw Mike walking back up the hill.

"You want me to rewind and see why he turned back?"

"No need. He was only out for a walk anyway. So, he would have to turn back somewhere." They kept watching Mike. He was walking up the hill, when the blacked-out truck passed him again.

"This doesn't add up. Why is that guy driving up and down the hill."

"Maybe he is lost." Said Billy.

"There are a couple of properties up this way, including this one. Not a place to be lost."

They watched as the truck pulled to the side of the road. The driver got out, walked round to the other side and bent down next to one of the wheels. After a minute, he stood up and walked to the back of the truck. He pulled out a jack, a tyre Iron, and a spare wheel.

"Did he just let his own tyre down?" asked Billy.

"It certainly looked like it to me."

They watched as the truck guy got to work with the jack. Moments later, Mike walked into view. They watched the guy look in Mike's direction, and saw him mouth something.

"I think he's asking Mike for some help."

"Forward it again."

Billy forwarded the camera feed and watched as Mike and the truck guy got to work changing the wheel in a faster speed than normal. Mike picked up the old wheel and walked to the back of the truck, with the guy following him with the jack. The guy put the jack in the back of the truck, then moved out of the way to let Mike put the wheel in. After putting the wheel in the back, Mike suddenly put his hands kind of half in the air. Mike then walked around the side of the truck with the guy following closely behind. Then the guy suddenly raised his arm and Mike was then lying on the floor.

"Stop. Back it up a bit." Said Stan. "Ok, stop there. Now play in normal speed."

They watched as the truck guy stepped out of the way for Mike to get the wheel in the back. Once Mike put the wheel in the truck, both men walked round the side of the truck, then it looked like the guy hit Mike over the head, knocking him to the ground.

"Son of a bitch." Said Stan. "what did he just hit him with?"

Billy rewound the recording and they watched again.

"Looks like he had something poked in his back before he was hit."

"I agree. Looks like he was instructing him to do something before he hit him."

"Looks like the tyre Iron to me." Said Billy.

"Yes, I agree. Zoom in on the licence plate."

Billy zoomed in on the licence plate.

"It's a San Francisco plate."

"Ok. Get this licence owner tracked down. Mike is in the Shit, and we need to get him out of wherever he is."

141

50

I stood there catching my breath. I couldn't hold my foot. I couldn't dance around. Just had to stay still, taking the pain. I felt, if I gritted my teeth any harder, I would break them all. I took deep breaths, closed my eyes, and tried to focus on something else. Nick stood in front of me, just staring, with that bloody grin on his face. If I could get my hands on that hammer right now, I'd smash his face with it. He started pacing around the basement like he was thinking. I started to work the rope up and down again. I couldn't work it too much as they had tied my arms tighter when they stood me up.

"You ready to talk now?" said Nick.

"Screw you." I said, through gritted teeth.

He walked over to me, and without a word, just stood on my squashed toe. I screamed with my mouth closed trying to stifle it gritting my teeth harder. I think I felt one crack, but I was to focused on the pain. Nick left the room, I was alone again. This was just the beginning; I wasn't sure how much I had to endure. But I knew it would get worse. I kept working on my bonds, at the same time trying to work my leg bonds loose. I really wanted to sit down and take the weight off my arms and legs, but this was done so I would be uncomfortable.

It felt like an hour later when Nick came back. He didn't have the smug look anymore. He looked serious.

"We don't have time to mess around anymore." He said.

"We are going to take out your friends and get Carol back. I wanted to have my fun with you, but unfortunately, I no longer have that luxury. So, I'm going to leave you in the capable hands of my two friends here. They will keep you company while I'm away. Hopefully there will be something left of you to punish, when I return."

"I look forward to it" I said.

He walked over to me and punched me in the gut. I would have puked if I'd had any food in me. It didn't stop me gagging. He hit me again. I couldn't double over and protect myself. He hit me a third time, then punched me hard in the face. I must have really pissed him off. I came round, probably a few minutes later, as one of the guys threw cold water over me. Nick was gone, but his goons stood there smiling at me. One of them was a small slim guy. Shaved head, stubble face, about five feet nothing. His buddy was a few inches taller, and looked like he liked his food. Another shaved head, with a full beard.

"We are going to enjoy this." Said the smaller guy.

I had the feeling; he was the one in charge. He told his big friend to have some fun, then he left the room. Shit. This isn't wasn't to be pleasant.

51

"Any sign of Mike's phone tracker?" asked Stan.

"Nothing at all. It must be switched off."

"Shit. Can't you track it while it's off?"

"It depends if the location was switched on but normally it goes down when the phone is off."

"Try anyway. We need to do all we can to get him back. In the meantime, I will get Carol brought down here. It's the safest place in the house."

"You expecting trouble?"

"Just want to be prepared. If it happens, we need her safe. If they get her back, we won't see her again. You up for some female company?"

"Somehow I don't think I have a choice."

"That's the spirit" said Stan smiling.

 Stan left, to arrange for Carol to be brought down. Billy continued to try and locate Mike's phone position. He got an alert on one of his screens, telling him that the computer had found the address where the blacked-out truck is registered. And the registered owner. He called Stan.

 "What ya got, Billy?"

"Boss, I have an address in San Jose, for the truck and its owner."

"Good man. Send it to me, and I'll get some lads over there."

"Sending it now boss."

Stan walked through the house to his office. He called Danny, and asked him to join him. It wasn't long before he was at the office.

"Ah, Danny. Can you get a couple of guys over to this address, find out where they have Mike? This guy was the one who bundled Mike and took him away. Do whatever it takes to get answers. If this guy isn't home yet, tell the guys to wait for him."

"Yes boss. I'll get on it."

"One more thing. Once you've sorted that, can you arrange for Carol to go down to Billy's. He knows she is coming, any provisions she needs while she is down there, make sure she gets them. She may be down there for a little while."

"Will do. Do you want men on the door?" said Danny.

"Yes. Good idea. Put a couple of guys down there."

Danny left the office, and went about his tasks. Stan sat there looking out of the window. "Where are you, Mike? Where are you?"

52

The guy was staring at me. I could see in his eyes that he was looking forward to hurting me.

"How about, you untie me, and let me go. I'll get you a job on my side. Good pay. Good benefits." I said.

"You think this is funny? You won't be laughing soon."

I was still trying to weaken my bonds. He kept looking at the small toolbox on the bench. If he gets something from there it wouldn't be good.

"Oi, come on, untie me. Let's have a proper fight."

I was trying to take his mind off the toolbox. He walked over and punched me in the gut. I nearly puked, it took everything just to get my breath back. At least he'd stopped looking at the box of tools. I needed to get hold of him, there may be something on his person, I could use to get free. I kept trying to loosen my leg bonds, they were slowly working loose.

"I gotta take a leak." I said.

"Then take a leak."

"Come on mate. You aren't going to make me piss myself, are you?"

"I don't give a shit, if you piss yourself or not. You need to piss, then piss."

"Under different circumstances I'd beat the crap out of you." I said.

The guy walked round behind me, put his arm around the post and my neck and started to put pressure on my throat, he was trying to choke me. I started wriggling my legs like crazy, it was hurting, but I needed to get my legs out, my vision was starting to get starry. I didn't know how far he was going to go, so I needed to get free. My legs were working overtime now, I was frantically pulling at the rope, it looked like I was cycling on the spot. Finally, the rope was loose enough for me to pull one leg out, it took a lot of effort, but I managed to get it free. I was starting to feel really sleepy now, he was winning. I got my foot free, then quickly pulled the other one free. I was throwing my feet round behind me, trying to hit him. I connected with his legs a few times. I felt like I was about to pass out, when he let go. He'd obviously realised I was getting free. He came round to the front of me and tried to get my legs bound again. I kept kicking out, preventing him from doing it. He eventually got really angry and jumped at my legs and grabbed the rope. He had a good grip; he was a strong guy. I wriggled and got me legs free, this time I got my legs round his neck. I had to do this really quick, and not relax my legs for a second. My head was still fuzzy, but I had to put him down. I gripped his neck with my legs and crossed them, bringing him towards me and pulling on his throat. He started punching my legs hard,

I was obviously putting pressure on him. He was starting to panic now, he started trying to call for his mate, but didn't really get his words out. I was struggling to keep a tight hold on him, my legs were on fire with the effort, but I needed to keep going. he was slowing down now; he'd stopped hitting my legs. I was winning. I Just needed to keep going, just a little longer. He finally went still, I gave his neck a final big squeeze, then slowly relaxed my legs. I kept them round his neck for a few moments, just in case he wasn't completely out. Now I just needed to see if he had anything useful on him, then figure out how to get my arms free, before his mate came back.

53

Stan was in his office looking at some paperwork, when his phone rang.

"Yes, Billy."

"Boss, I have an address for Mike's phone tracker."

"Give it to me."

"It's in the Hollywood Hills. Franklin Canyon park."

"Is that where they took, Mike?"

"It's where the tracker ends. They must have found his phone and switched it off."

"Ok, I'll get some guys over there to look around. Good job, Billy."

Stan called Danny and told him to take some guys over to Franklin Canyon park and have a look around, see if there was any sign if where Mike may be.

"Shall I call back the guys going up to check out the truck guy?" said Danny.

"No, let them carry on. If you and your men find anything, we can call them back. We may still need them to get us an address from him. Although, he might not be there anyway if he stayed where they have Mike."

"We'll head over there now."

Stan went down to Billy's basement in time to see Carol being settled in.

"Ah, you have everything you need? I hope." Said Stan.

"Yes, I am being looked after well." Said Carol. "Although, I feel bad for Billy sleeping on the couch"

"He wouldn't have it any other way. Do you know if your husband has, or had any property at Franklin canyon park?"

"Not that I know of. Is that where he is?"

"We believe he has one of our friends held up there."

"He has lots of properties. He has a few here in LA, but mainly in San Francisco. I don't know of all of his places, so, it's possible." Said Carol.

"We're looking into it anyway."

"What are you going to do to him?"

"We want the evidence to put him away. His cousin Nick, is the main problem right now. Once we've dealt with him, we can then deal with Rufus. He needs to be put away for what he has done, and we are going to make sure, that happens." Said Stan.

"Be careful with, Nick. He is a nasty piece of work."

"We know what he is capable of. We will deal with him however we need to."

"Well, nobody will miss him." Said Carol.

"Good to know."

"Boss. I have a location."

Stan rushed over to Billy. "Where is he? Billy showed Stan a house at Franklin Canyon park. "I managed to hack into Mike's phone and get a ping on where he is."

"How accurate is the location?"

"This location is exactly where Mike's phone is. Chances are, he is there too."

"Can you get a real-time view of the house?"

"Yes, to within a minute. Best I can do."

"You are a star, Billy. Ping this location over to Danny. I'll call him and talk to him."

"Yes boss." Said Danny.

"Billy just sent you a location, we are pretty sure this is where they have Mike. That Nick character is there, so be careful. Danny, we need to get Mike out of there, no matter what. Do what you have to do."

"Will do boss."

The call ended, and Stan went back to Billy.

"This is the real-time feed, well, within a minute. But I'll keep watching and I'll be able to see if anyone comes or goes."

"Good man. Let me know if anything changes."

Stan went back up to his office. He arranged for another team of guys to get over to the location as backup.

54

I spun myself round the column, so I could get back down on my arse, and root through the big guys pockets. I need anything with a rough edge so I could cut through the ropes. I'd managed to work them a little, but not enough to get free. All I could do Is rummage through and feel for anything useful. It wasn't ideal doing this behind my back. But It was my only option. He had some keys in his pocket, that was all. It was better than nothing. I got to work.

 Danny and his guys were in the area. Now they had a location, they would be there in less than a minute.

"Ok guys. Myself and Ryan will go in the front. You two go round the back. Anyone tries to leave, take them down. Quietly if possibly. It's an empty neighbourhood, but one or two of these properties are still occupied. If it goes noisy, take em down quick. Stan is sending another team this way. We don't know how many are in there so, keep your eyes peeled. Let's get Mike out of there and get back. Ok let's go."

 I was still working on the ropes, when the door opened. then it went to shit. The small boss guy came running over to check his mate, realising he was dead, he launched himself at me. He started kicking and punching me, then went for my throat. This wasn't good. I dropped the keys. All I could do was try and pull my arms out before he killed me. They were tied good. He was squeezing the crap out of me. I knew it wouldn't be long before I passed out, then it would be all over. I'd stopped trying to get my arms free. I was too weak. I was moments away from passing out. All thoughts of survival had gone. I knew these were my last moments. There was nothing I could do to stop it happening. Then my face suddenly felt wet, then it all went dark.

Danny and Ryan went through the house clearing it. The other two guys took the upstairs. It was all clear, there didn't seem to be anyone around. They continued until they all met in the downstairs hallway again. There was one more door to check. They slowly opened the door, and it led down some stairs.

"Basement" Ryan whispered.

They walked down the stairs cautiously, they led to another door that was open. Ryan was first in the doorway, and he could see an empty room, with a smooth concrete column in the middle with someone tied to it. He could tell it was me. Danny followed closely behind and as soon as he saw what was happening he ran into the room and put a bullet in the head of the guy who had his hands round my throat. He grabbed me, and tried to bring me round. my breathing was shallow, but I was alive. They got me untied, then laid me down. I was still out. they kept trying to bring me round, then eventually I opened my eyes. Danny called Stan and told him what was happening. Once I was back with it again, they carried me out to the vehicle, and headed home.

55

I laid on my bed, my throat was sore. Danny had told me what had happened. I owed him my life. My throat was still a little swollen, but I could swallow well enough, to get some water in me. I'd been in situations before, where I thought I would have my last moments, but nothing like that. That was as close to dying as I planned to get for a while. Whilst they were sorting me out, Billy had found out that Nick had a plan to attack the house and get Carol back. I don't know how he finds his information, but he is a genius, and he basically saved my skin by getting the guys to my location. At this point I'd believe anything he told me. We assumed Nick would try something like this, but now it had been confirmed, we could act on it. Carol was safe in the basement, with Billy. No one was going to get in there, especially now there were men guarding the place. Stan had men take up positions around the property, ready to act. It was just a waiting game now. There were enough cameras here to spot anyone up to no good, so the chances of him getting in here, were slim. For two days we just kept an eye on things. My throat was better now. The guy's Stan had sent to have a word with black truck man, were called back. We were getting ready to eat a late supper, when Billy told Stan he needed to see him ASAP. I went with him to see Billy.

"Boss. We have someone at the front gate, making a scene. I've instructed security to get rid of him, but he refuses to leave."

"Zoom in on him."

Billy zoomed in on the man, but none of us recognised him.

"This is a distraction." I said.

We stood there looking at all of the camera feeds. There was no one around, apart from our security teams.

"We need to be ready now." Said Stan.

Stan and I left, and Stan instructed the guys on the door to let no one, but us in. We ran up to the main part of the house and checked that all the teams were in place. Billy was still watching the camera feeds. The guy at the front gate had just walked away after giving the security guys the finger. It was about two minutes later when the three security guys at the front gate, were suddenly covered in smoke, then a group of armed men rushed through, taking out the security guys as they went. The hut was full of smoke but Billy knew what had happened. The property was now under attack. He hit a red button on his computer console and an alarm sounded. Now everyone knew it had started. I convinced Stan to go down to Billy's place. Two of our teams engaged the armed men as they got nearer the house. It was on, we were now in a fight to protect the property, and everyone in it. Billy's cameras were showing men running all over the place. Their men, our men. A total clusterfuck. We didn't know how many there were, but they were coming from all angles. The house suddenly rattled with a massive explosion. One end of the house turned into debris, as it blew to pieces. What the hell were they using to do this.

 We lost a few men through that explosion, and the armed men were still coming. Billy was talking through our ear pieces, telling us were they were heading, and warning us to be ready. Another big bang at the back of the house. At first, I thought they had used RPG's, but these bangs were too big for that. It was more like explosives. At this moment it seemed that they were winning this fight.

56

My soul mission, was to find Nick. He was here somewhere, I knew it. Once I had dealt with him, I could concentrate on other things. Mainly, helping Carol out with Rufus. And checking in on Sally and the girls. I caught up with Danny and Ryan. We went through the house, clearing the rooms. We left Billy's part of the house, to the security down there. We wanted to clear the house then get outside. once we'd managed to clear the house, we worked our way outside. Still a lot of gunfire out here. One of their guys was lying injured on the ground, so I grabbed him and asked him where Nick was, he just told me to get lost. His world went dark. We fought our way through the main gardens towards the out buildings. I knew Nick was hiding out here somewhere. He liked to blow people up, but be nearby to watch the carnage. We came up to the first of the small buildings, it was a small brick and corrugated shed. We split up, I went to go in the front, Danny and Ryan went to the back. I crept in slowly through the partially open door. And to my surprise, Nick was sitting on an upturned bucket, with some kind of small computer device in his hands.

"Ah, Mike. Finally. I was wondering how long it would take you to find me. I thought I'd make it easy for you, and wait in the first building. You can be quite predictable."

"You do know, you won't be walking out of here." I said.

"Oh, I think I will. You see, I have the upper hand here, Mike."

As if to prove his point, Danny walked into the back of the shed with Ryan's gun pointing at him.

"Ryan, what the fuck?" I said.

"Sorry Mike, but Nick here, offered me a bigger bank balance. How could I refuse."

"You've made a rod for your own back. You won't make it out of here."

"I know how you lot operate, Mike. Yes, we had to plan this quickly. But while you were hanging around in that basement, I was getting things ready here. We have explosives planted around the property, and we will take Carol out of here, like it or not."

"You idiot. Do you really think that you will succeed, and get out of here?"

"I don't think, Mike. I know. Now put your gun down and sit over there."

He pointed to a crate, the other side of the shed.

"I don't think so" I said.

Ryan pushed his weapon onto the back of Danny's head.

"I won't ask again."

I could tell, he was ready to put a bullet in Danny, so I slowly put my weapon on the floor, and walked over to the crate, not taking my eyes off him.

"Let him go. He doesn't need to be here."

"Always the hero, Mike."

He pushed Danny over towards where I was sitting. Danny sat down next to me.

"Now you two are comfortable, you can watch our little show."

Nick turned the device round to face us.

"Now you will see how we intend to win this."

We were looking at the screen. He had somehow hacked into the property's camera feeds. We were looking at the main hallway outside Stan's office. There were security guys standing outside the office door, And others posted along the hallway. Nick pressed a button on the screen, a split second later the hallway and office erupted into a great fire ball.

"Son of a bitch" I shouted. I went to launch myself at Nick, but Ryan shot at the ground in front of me. I stopped before I'd even started. My blood was boiling, I wanted nothing more than to get hold of him, and make him suffer. I realised that they hadn't noticed that we were wearing ear pieces, so I started to say things I hoped Billy would cotton on to.

"They will track us down. They will realise that we are in this little corrugated shed, and they will come and take you down." I said.

57

Billy sat at his computer, listening in to the radio chatter. There was a lot of noise because all the guys were communicating at the same time, over the gun fire. Billy thought he could hear me having a conversation out of the ordinary. He turned down the feed to all radios except mine. He heard me talking about the shed out back. He quickly realised that I was telling him where we were, and we obviously needed assistance. He was trying to contact the teams, to come and help us, as soon as he made contact with someone, they seemed to suddenly disappear. He thought the explosions had something to do with it. Stan was getting pissed off. His office was gone. Half the house was disappearing.

"We need to end this, before there is nothing left."

"I'm trying to contact the teams to help Mike and Danny. but they are getting wiped out quick."

"Message them all on their phones, tell them all to split up and surround that shed. We have enough protection down here. They are all safer out of the house now anyway. He is taking this place apart, piece by piece. The men need to get out."

"On it." Said Billy.

"If he has tapped into some of our systems, there is nothing to say he hasn't tapped into our radio's." Said Stan.

"Done. Let's hope they see them, and don't all ignore their phones right now."

They watched the screens as some of the men looked at their phones. Word soon got round what they needed to do. The guys who had checked their phones started to round up the other guys.

"It's working boss. They are all heading over to the shed."

"We can assume that Nick is in there. He obviously has men in there with him, so we need to be careful. We need to get Mike and Danny out safely."

"Tell the teams to spread out around the shed, in two layers."

The message was sent, and they could see the teams forming into two tiers. If one tier started taking fire, the rear tier could fight on through.

"Ask all the guys to ditch their ear pieces, apart from team leaders."

The teams done as asked and ditched their ear pieces. Just the team leaders had them now. One of the team leaders was asked to get the attention of Nick and his men. Once he got their attention, he was to make sure they got one of the ear pieces.

"NICK." One of the men shouted. You are to have one of these." He held up an ear piece.

"They have surrounded us. They want you to have an ear piece." Said Ryan.

"I knew they'd want to talk eventually. Get them to throw one over."

"Throw one over." Shouted Ryan.

The team leader threw an ear piece over to the doorway at the back of the shed. Ryan picked it up and threw it to Nick. It was a small ear piece with a throat mic attached.

"Who wants to chat?" Nick said into the mic.

"I do." Said Stan. "you need to give up now. If you continue with this, your lives won't be spared."

"I think you will find; I will be giving the orders. We will be taking Carol back, so make it easier on yourselves and hand her over."

"Now you know we can't do that. She is staying. Even if you take this whole house down. You won't get to her."

"I think you under estimate your situation. We have the whole place wired. Once we find your little hideout, we'll take that down too."

"You can't blast your way in without harming Carol. You wouldn't be going through all of this, just to risk killing her in the process." Said Stan.

"You don't know what we are capable of." Said Nick.

"The way I see it is, the only men you have, are the ones in there with you. We've taken out the rest. So, you are outnumbered, out gunned, and out of options."

"Stan just kill this, son of a bitch." I shouted down my mic.

"We won't hesitate to storm the building. My guys in there know how this works. We will take you down. Now just come out and let's end this."

Another explosion erupted somewhere in what was left of the house. Stan was getting more pissed off with his house getting blown to bits, but he kept his cool.

"We can just as easily sit and wait for you to finish blowing up all of your little gadgets. Then we will come in and take you down. Stop being a fool."

"I'm no fool." Shouted Nick.

He pulled off the mic and threw it across the other side of the shed. Stan was getting to him. He knew it was the best way to get someone to make a mistake. Keep pulling on his strings and he would fuck up eventually.

58

Nick started pressing buttons on his handheld device. Parts of the property started to blow to bits.

"Son of a bitch" said Stan.

They watched the cameras, as explosions rang out around the house. Stan was thankful that he got all the guys out of the house. He knew the house would end up destroyed. Stan radioed his men.

"Can we confirm how many are in that shed with, Mike and Danny?"

"Not yet boss. We've only had eyes on the one I threw the ear piece to."

"I can help with that boss." Said Billy.

He pressed some keys on his keyboard, and a camera feed came up. It was showing a small area on the roof of an out building. They soon heard a buzzing sound, and Stan realised it was a drone.

"What you gonna do with that?" he asked.

"I'll show you." Said Billy.

He flew the drone up out of where it was, and flew in the direction of the shed. Once he got near it, he hit another key on his keyboard. The camera feed went dark, aside from light sources around the property. It detected heat, so, it soon picked up their men standing around the outside of the shed. Billy flew it over to one side of the shed and hovered there, pointing the camera at the shed wall. The feed showed, four heat sources, two were sat together on one side of the space, one was standing near the rear doorway, and one was sat on his own.

"I'd say the two sitting there are Mike and Danny. The one standing, has to be one of their gunmen, so Nick would be the one sat by himself. Looks like he's holding something in his hands. Must be what he is using to set off those explosions.

"There can't be many more, they haven't been here long." Said Stan.

"I'd say, looking at what's left of the house, he must be finished with the fireworks."

"I'd like to think so. Let's assume he hasn't for now. Can you do anything about that man on the door? If we can take him out, Nick will be out numbered."

"That I can do."

He hovered the drone near the wall behind where Ryan was standing near the doorway. He brought up a target screen and aimed it at the spot between Ryan's shoulder blades. They got a message through from one of the team leaders.

"Boss, so you know, Ryan is the one we tossed the ear piece to. He is no longer with us."

"Damn it." Said Stan. "he's made his choice."

"Ok Billy. Do it."

59

Danny and I were sat there, waiting for what was going to happen next, then it happened. One-minute Ryan was standing near the doorway, the next he was falling to the floor wit blood spraying out from his chest. They'd shot him in the back, blowing a hole out of his chest. I threw myself towards Nick. I dived on him before he realised what was happening. He dropped the device he was holding, and I started pounding him. By the time Danny pulled me off him, my hand was already aching. I'd hit him so many times in a short space of time, he wasn't going to be fighting back this time. Danny let the guys outside know that it was over. A couple of the guys came into the shed to check on us.

"Tie this piece of shit up." I said. pointing to Nick.

One of the guys tied him up with plastic ties.

"I'll deal with him in a minute. Don't let him out of your sight."

I stepped outside and told a couple more guys to watch over Nick. Stan had come out to see us. There wasn't much left of the house. I could see the stress on Stan's face as he walked towards us.

"Thank god you are both safe." He said as he shook both of our hands.

"We lose many? I asked.

"A dozen or so. But we need to check. The basement is untouched. As you can see, most of the house was destroyed."

"You can rebuild yeah?"

"Don't know. We will have to look at that once we've cleaned up. What are you going to do with him?" Stan said. Pointing to the shed.

"I'm going to repay a debt." I said.

I turned round and walked back to the shed. I told the guys watching Nick to go outside. He was sitting with his back against a wall.

"I was going to make you suffer. But I don't want to look at you any longer than I have to. I told you, you weren't getting out of here alive. I've been waiting for this moment you piece of shit."

Nick said nothing, just spat blood onto the floor. I walked over and knelt down in front of him. I pulled the knife from my thigh holster.

"I'm going to enjoy this."

I put the tip of the knife against his throat, and very slowly pushed the blade into his flesh. It started to cut into him and he started to gag. His eyes went wide.

174

"Fuck you." I said as I pushed the blade further into him. He was gurgling now. Blood was trickling from his mouth as well as his throat. His eyes were starting to glaze over.

"That's for my friend John."

I stood up, put my foot against the end of the knife handle, and pushed it in hard.

60

"What's the plan now?" I asked Stan.

"I guess we rebuild the house. I kind of like this place, I will get temporary cabins out here to keep a roof over our heads until its finished."

"What about Rufus?"

"Billy is working on finding the evidence. If that evidence was found on the web, he will find it again. Then we can get Rufus where he belongs. Then get Carol settled, so she can move on."

"And until then?"

"I guess we can all just relax a while, until then."

"I'm going back to London for a few days." I said. "I have a few things to get cleared up."

"Anything you need, you let us know. Billy will book your flights. Have you given anymore thought about what Danny said?"

"What was that.?"

"You staying here and working with us."

"I haven't thought about it to be honest."

"Then get thinking, we could use you here. You will be looked after, you know that."

"I'll think about it while I'm away."

"Good man, let Billy know what you need. See you when you get back."

Stan walked away, smiling.

I went to see Billy, and told him what flights I needed. He booked me on a flight the following day. Danny told me he would take me to the airport. I went and packed a few things, I planned to pack, get freshened up and go for something to eat. I was looking forward to a change of scenery.

61

I landed in London Heathrow the following day. I went back to my apartment to get freshened up. I was happy to see that the friend i had asked to pick my car up at the airport had not let me down. After getting sorted and getting a coffee down my neck, I set off to see Sally. I was expecting a cold reception. I parked my car, and walked to the front door. It opened before I got there.

"Mike" said Sally, as she opened the door.

"Hi"

She let me in, and went to make a brew.

"I was wondering when you were going to show up."

"Sorry. I had things to attend to."

"More important than being here for John's memorial?"

"I'm sorry, Sally. I had to find the guy who killed John."

"Was it worth it?"

"I got him, Sally. The son of a bitch is dead."

"And that makes it all better, does it?"

"No, of course not, but he can't hurt anyone else. She didn't say anything.

"How are the girls doing?"

"How do you think they are doing, they have lost their father."

I didn't have an answer for that.

"I'd like to see the memorial."

She wrote down the address, and handed me the piece of paper. I handed her an envelope. It was something John asked me to give to her in the event he never made it home.

"What's this?"

"John asked me to give you this, in the event he didn't make it home."

"He knew he might not come home?"

"No No, he gave me this a few years ago, just in case anything ever happened to him."

"I'm thinking of going away."

"I'm glad you can think of holidays right now."

"Not holiday, I'm thinking of moving away. Why don't you and the girls come with me."

"Really? John is recently dead, and you want to take me away. You've changed, Mike."

"Not to stay with me. Just be nearby in case you need anything. The girls would love it there. You wouldn't see me unless you needed to."

"Where exactly?"

"L.A."

"You mean Los Angeles? Are you mad? The girls are settled here. And we just had John's memorial. I'm not about to move away now."

"We can set up a new memorial. I will help you and the girls get settled."

"No, Mike."

"Well, if you change your mind. Let me know."

"That's not going to happen, Mike."

"Anything I can do before I go?"

"No. We are fine thanks."

"Call me if you need me."

I left their house and drove to the address for John's memorial. It was in a small village church. John's memorial was on the edge of the grave yard, alongside a few other memorials.

John's memorial was beautiful, A marble headstone with his picture on it. The whole thing looked amazing. I paid my respects and just stood there for a few minutes. He was my best friend, like a brother. He will be missed. I left the church yard and went back to my apartment and got my head down.

62

I woke the next morning feeling better about things. I'd laid awake most of the night thinking about my next move. I had nothing to stay in London for. John was gone., Sally and the girls were sorted, they didn't need me hanging around. It was time to move on. I spent the next couple of days, putting my apartment on the market, and just getting rid of things I didn't need. I could find a nine to five job, and just plod along, but that's not me. Working with Stan and the boys will keep things exciting for me. I get bored easily, so I need to keep active. I booked a flight back to L.A. and made my way to the airport. It was a late flight, but that was fine with me. I could hopefully catch up on sleep and get ready for a fresh start. At least the airport was reasonably quiet this late in the day. It would be around two in the morning once I touched down in L.A. I booked myself a hotel for a few nights. With most of Stan's guys sleeping in cabins until the house was rebuilt, I thought it easier to stay somewhere out of the way. When I eventually landed in L.A, I picked up a hire car, and made my way to the hotel. I wasn't really tired, since I'd slept on the plane, so after booking in I went to an all-night bar, had a couple of drinks, and reflected on the last few weeks. Things had happened fast. I'd lost friends, made new friends. Once Rufus was dealt with, this would be done. I wasn't sure what life would bring in the near future, but for now I would just do what I do, and see where it leads. I received a message from Stan, telling me that Billy had found more evidence on the Rufus case, but he wasn't sure if it would be enough to put him away. They had tried to get some duplicates of the original evidence, but that just didn't happen. I couldn't believe that he might get away with what he'd done. We would just have to make sure that he didn't get near Carol ever again. I messaged Stan back, and told him I would be there in the morning. I went back to the hotel, showered, and got my head down. The next morning, I got myself sorted then went to find some coffee and breakfast. After filling myself up, I went to get my car then headed over to Stan's. He was all smiles when I got there, despite the state of the place.

"Good to see you, Mike."

"You too." I said, as we shook hands.

I followed him down to Billy's basement.

"I hope all is well back home?" said Stan.

"No reason for me to be there now. Nothing for me in London." I said.

"Does this mean you are staying" he said with a smirk.

"I guess it does." I said.

"Excellent news. You won't regret it."

"I hope not" I said.

63

184

Billy showed us what he had found, and it wasn't concrete evidence.

"This isn't enough to put that piece of shit away." I said.

"That's what we were thinking." Said Billy

"Problem is, if we try, and fail. He walks free."

"Then what do you suggest?" said Stan.

"Get rid of him. Make it look like an accident, Carol gets everything. Job done."

"For someone who didn't even want a gun, a while back, you have certainly changed."

"It's the only way to end this. I've lost friends, and you've lost men because of him. I'm sure she won't miss him."

I nodded towards Carol; she was sat watching TV.

"Maybe she won't. But if this goes wrong, she could lose everything."

"Then let's make sure it doesn't go wrong." I said.

"What do you suggest we do?"

"We make him sign everything over to Carol. Then get rid of him." Said Billy.

"That would look suspicious if he signs everything over to her, then disappears."

"Then make it look like suicide, leave a note, signing everything over to her."

"I'm pretty sure it needs to be done before he dies."

"We could just empty his bank. Who cares what happens to his properties. She will have enough to start over and to have a good life."

"That's actually not a bad idea" I said.

"Well, I guess it's time to pay him a visit." Said Stan. First thing in the morning, we head up there and end this."

"I need to eat, I'm heading out to get something."

"No need Mike. We have caterers here, very good caterers."

"Well then, lead the way."

On the way to the canteen that was set up in the grounds, Stan told me what his plans were for the new place. Bigger and better was pretty much was he had in mind. Even adding a good size place for me. He was building a self-contained annex at the back of the main house.

"What if I'd decided not to stay?"

"Don't give me that. You were always going to stay. You just didn't know it."

We both laughed as we walked into the canteen. Once we'd eaten, I left. Heading back to my hotel, I decided to stop for a drink before calling it a day.

I eventually made it to my hotel room, a little wobbly on my feet. I needed to relax and have a drink, but I had more than I needed. I got showered then got my head down, ready for the day ahead.

64

The next morning, I went over to Stan's. He had two teams ready to go and he was also dressed ready for action.

"You planning on joining us?" I said.

"After all that's happened, I want to see the end of all this."

"Fair enough. Can't argue with that."

"Danny has your gear ready down at Billy's."

I walked down to Billy's basement, he was sat at his computers as usual. Danny was checking over his own gear.

"Morning, Mike. You think we will need all this?"

"After our last visit to Rufus's house, I'd say it's better safe than sorry."

"Yeah, the welcoming committee. They didn't fair to well did they."

"We know what to expect this time. We go in, hard and fast. This ends today."

"Yeah it does."

After checking our gear. We headed back to the vehicles.

It was going to be a long day. Once we got up there, we we're going to go straight in. He won't be expecting it, he won't be ready for it.

"Ok guys. Once we get there, we will be going in. We are going to pull up and get in fast. Let's not give them a chance to react. Once we get hold of Rufus, we will do what needs doing, then get out of there. We finish this today. Then we can concentrate on other things. Keep your eyes and ears open. We all come home today. Everyone happy with what they need to do?"

There was a thumbs up from the teams.

"Ok good. Let's go."

We all got our seats and set off. Maybe one day I'll have a nice walk in the Berkeley hills, but for now, as usual. It was business.

65

A knock at the door.

"Come in." Said Rufus.

"Sorry to bother you boss, but we've just seen two vehicles leaving the house where Carol is being held. At least four or five men in each."

"keep an eye on them. Track them. If they are coming this way, we will be ready. They won't get near the house this time."

"Will do boss."

After the guy left his office, Rufus called up his head of security.

"Make sure your teams know what they need to do. I want the perimeter well-guarded. They over ran us last time, we cannot let that happen again. They must not reach this house. Do you understand?"

"Yes boss. I will get the teams ready. They won't get through this time."

Rufus sat in his office chair. Whisky in one hand, cigar in the other. Since the last attack on his house, he'd moved all of his important papers out, and locked them in a secure location. They'd killed his cousin Nick, so they were obviously after him for Carol. She had obviously told them about her father, now they clearly want to put him away. He wasn't about to let that happen. He'd got away with it for all these years. He wasn't planning on it ending now. The Berkeley hills were his home. He planned to stay there. He wasn't about to let his wife get her hands on his wealth. He was brought back to reality by his door being knocked.

"What now."

"Sorry boss. It looks like they are heading north out of L.A."

"Ok. They could be here in seven or eight hours. I want your teams ready in position, now. Get them ready. Remember, they do not get near this house."

"On it boss."

"And get my helicopter ready."

He planned on getting the hell out of there if it went bad. He could easily escape it all, but he wanted to see Mike and his friends taken down.

66

I'd had a nap in the vehicle on the way up to San Francisco, now it was time to focus. We were a few minutes out and we needed to be ready to get this done. My mobile phone started to ring.

"Mike, we have word that Rufus has set up an assault team to protect the property. They are armed to the teeth."

"Ok. We'll bear that in mind."

"You need to hit them hard."

"Don't worry, Billy. We have this under control. Thanks for letting us know."

I relayed the message to Stan and the guys.

"Remember guys. We need to take Rufus alive. But, if he poses you a direct threat, take him down. Only shoot to kill as a last resort." Said Stan.

"Right guys, we are coming up to our drop off point. Let's get this done. Watch your backs. Don't get killed. We jumped out of our vehicles, and went straight for the tree line. We all knew what we were going to be doing, we all had our own roles to play. But ultimately, we needed to watch each other's backs. We split into three teams, Stan, Danny, and myself, and two other teams of three guys. We sent out the first team ahead, because they had a sniper with them. We knew we were up against it. And we knew we were undoubtedly, outnumbered. We followed up after a couple of minutes. The team with the sniper would head straight towards the front of the property. We would go round to the right, the other team would go left. We heard over the radio that the team we sent round to the left of the property had spotted a helicopter out to the side of the house.

"You need to get over there and render that thing useless. Quietly."

"On it."

"Do it quick, then get back to the property. We need you there."

"Will do."

We heard that the sniper team had four men in their sights, at the front door.

"Wait until I give the go ahead. Once the heli is dealt with, we can go in as one. We got ourselves into position, and waited. It was a ten-minute wait but we eventually heard back.

"Heli, taken care of, had to put two men down."

"We are about to let loose at the front of the house once the first man goes down, do what you need to."

"Roger that."

"Ok, the guys at the front are all yours. We go on your mark."

We didn't hear anything for a few seconds. We knew we wouldn't hear the rifle shots because it was a silenced weapon.

"Two down, other two running. Go Go."

We were off, we headed straight for the nearest entrance at the side of the house. We started getting fired upon, but we couldn't tell where it was coming from. We ducked down and carried on towards the side door, hoping to get out of the way of the bullets whizzing around us. I had a couple of close calls, as bullets pinged off brick work next to me. We let off some short bursts in the direction the incoming fire was coming from. That helped momentarily but it started straight up again. Danny got grazed on his leg. He could carry on. We got to the door and barged our way in. Someone shot at us from inside the house, but he soon got taken down by Stan when he went to try again. By this point the other teams were inside. One team had spotted Rufus running to the helicopter with three of his men. We worked our way through the property, only meeting with light resistance.

Billy had said they were armed to the teeth. We hadn't seen that yet. We knew this would get worse before it was over. The sniper team, lost a man due to an explosion. The other team were in a shootout with the men protecting Rufus. One of the team members was shot in the side. He was still going for it, so we assumed it wasn't really life threatening.

"Rufus is down. I repeat, Rufus is down."

Shit. I didn't want to hear that.

"Dead or alive?"

"Can't see from here. Will know soon."

"We are making our way to you."

67

We had gone pretty much from one side of the property to the other. Thinking we hadn't had much of a problem, we suddenly found ourselves thrown back with an intense heat of a big explosion. I was shaken awake by one if the sniper team guys. I had been out cold for a few minutes. He was talking to me, but I couldn't heart a word he was saying. My left ear was totally void of any noise and my right ear was ringing loudly. He pointed to me and gave a thumbs up, asking if I was ok. I pointed to my ears so he knew I couldn't hear then gave him a thumbs up to say I was otherwise ok. I looked to my right and saw Stan kneeling next to someone who was writhing around on the floor and screaming, it was Danny. He had a leg missing, and his other leg was at an unnatural angle. I tried to get up and help, but I was dizzy. Some other guys came over from one of the teams to help.

I eventually managed to shuffle my way over. Stan had burns to his face and hands. His clothes were partially burnt too. I looked down at my hands and realised I was burnt too. What the hell had they set off. The air was full of smoke. I tried to comfort Danny, but the pain was obviously too much. I told some of the guys to get him out of here, and get him medical attention. Stan helped me up, and we walked out towards the heli pad. Rufus was sat up against a small wall that surrounded the heli pad. At least he was still alive. I'd love nothing more at this point than to put a bullet in him, but we still needed him. He was dragged into his office and dumped in his office chair. I still couldn't hear anything, but I knew what he was now being asked to do. He wasn't happy about it, but he seemed to be doing what he was told to do. He was nothing without his men by his side. I watched as he was finally dragged back to the helicopter. He was put in the pilot's seat, and knocked out by a rifle butt to his head. Our guy who had knocked him out, pierced a hole in the fuel tank. He walked away to a safe distance. He turned, pulled out his side arm, and shot at the tank. After a couple of shots, the fuel ignited, causing the heli to burst into flames.

Rufus had been dealt with. We'd lost one of our guys. Danny was on his way to get medical help. I hoped he'd pull through; I liked the guy. The remainder of us headed back to our vehicle and set off for home.

68

The following morning, I woke, showered, then went for some breakfast. After eating and filling my coffee mug back up, I wandered off to see Stan. He was down at Billy's lair.

"We have word that Danny will be fine. Well, considering his injuries. They have fixed his broken leg, and we will make sure he gets the best prosthetics money can buy." Said Stan.

"That's good to hear."

"Carol has her money, so she can do whatever she needs to do now. I've offered her a place here, but she wants to move on. I've told her to contact us if she needs anything. She can stay here until she has everything sorted."

"It's been reported that an accident occurred up at the Berkeley hills. It's all gone down as an accident, just the way you wanted." Said Billy.

"That's good news. That means it will blow over soon enough."

"Just need to get this place back up and running again. Then we can get back to some sort of normality." I said.

"I need to change the plans now. This place needs to be fit for Danny to get around."

"If you mean, for a wheelchair, I don't think Danny is the type to sit around in one of those things."

"You're probably right. I can't see him doing that."

"So, what next?"

"What do you mean?"

"We have finally ended this, Rufus problem. Now what?"

"We carry on doing what we do. There is always someone out there, who needs our help. Question is; Are you still in?"

"Try and stop me."